Clint McPherson in the flesh.

He straightened suddenly, and she knew his instinct had warned him he was no longer alone. He swung around.

Brandy sensed two things immediately.

Her father had been right. Something was wrong. The light that had always flared in Clint's eyes, brilliant and fierce, had an element in it she did not understand. It was as if ice and fire battled within him, and ice was winning.

And the second thing she could not ignore was that her skin was tingling treacherously. She loved Clint McPherson in some primal way she was not sure she could ever tame.

Nonsense, she told herself, *utter hogwash.*

She had been taming the untamable her whole life!

She was here on assignment for her father. And herself. She would lay her childish heartbreaks and hopes to rest. She would see Clint McPherson through the eyes of a mature woman…and tame that thing inside her that *wanted* him.

Dear Reader,

Just as the seasons change, you may have noticed that our Silhouette Romance covers have evolved over the past year. We have tried to create cover art that uses more soft pastels, sun-drenched images and tender scenes to evoke the aspirational and romantic spirit of this line. We have also tried to make our heroines look like women you can relate to and may want to be. After all, this line is about the joys of falling in love, and we hope you can live vicariously through these heroines.

Our writers this month have done an especially fine job in conveying this message. Reader favorite Cara Colter leads the month with *That Old Feeling* (#1814) in which the heroine must overcome past hurts to help her first love raise his motherless daughter. This is the debut title in the author's emotional new trilogy, A FATHER'S WISH. Teresa Southwick concludes her BUY-A-GUY miniseries with the story of a feisty lawyer who finds herself saddled with an unwanted and wholly irresistible bodyguard, in *Something's Gotta Give* (#1815). A sister who'd do anything for her loved ones finds her own sweet reward when she switches places with her sibling, in *Sister Swap* (#1816)— a compelling new romance by Lilian Darcy. Finally, in *Made-To-Order Wife* (#1817) by Judith McWilliams, a billionaire hires an etiquette expert to help him land the perfect society wife, and he soon starts rethinking his marriage plans.

Be sure to return next month when Cara Colter continues her trilogy and Judy Christenberry returns to the line.

Happy reading!

Ann Leslie Tuttle
Associate Senior Editor

Please address questions and book requests to:
Silhouette Reader Service
U.S.: 3010 Walden Ave., P.O. Box 1325, Buffalo, NY 14269
Canadian: P.O. Box 609, Fort Erie, Ont. L2A 5X3

CARA COLTER

That Old Feeling

A Father's Wish

SILHOUETTE **Romance**®

Published by Silhouette Books

America's Publisher of Contemporary Romance

To Krista Casada, with thanks for all the "bubbles" you blow my way: friendship, inspiration, laughter.

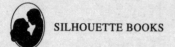 SILHOUETTE BOOKS

ISBN 0-373-19814-0

THAT OLD FEELING

Copyright © 2006 by Cara Colter

This edition published by arrangement with Harlequin Books S.A.

® and TM are trademarks of Harlequin Books S.A., used under license. Trademarks indicated with ® are registered in the United States Patent and Trademark Office, the Canadian Trade Marks Office and in other countries.

Visit Silhouette Books at www.eHarlequin.com

Printed in U.S.A.

Books by Cara Colter

Silhouette Romance

Dare To Dream #491
Baby in Blue #1161
Husband in Red #1243
*The Cowboy, the Baby
  and the Bride-to-Be* #1319
Truly Daddy #1363
A Bride Worth Waiting For #1388
Weddings Do Come True #1406
A Babe in the Woods #1424
A Royal Marriage #1440
First Time, Forever #1464
*Husband by Inheritance #1532
*The Heiress Takes a Husband #1538

*Wed by a Will #1544
What Child Is This? #1585
Her Royal Husband #1600
*9 Out of 10 Women Can't Be
  Wrong* #1615
*Guess Who's Coming for
  Christmas?* #1632
What a Woman Should Know
  #1685
Major Daddy #1710
Her Second-Chance Man #1726
Nighttime Sweethearts #1754
†That Old Feeling #1814

*The Wedding Legacy
†A Father's Wish

Silhouette Books

The Coltons
A Hasty Wedding

CARA COLTER

shares ten acres in the wild Kootenay region of British Columbia with the man of her dreams, three children, two horses, a cat with no tail and a golden retriever who answers best to "bad dog." She loves reading, writing and the woods in winter (no bears). She says life's delights include an automatic garage door opener and the skylight over the bed that allows her to see the stars at night. She also says, "I have not lived a neat and tidy life, and used to envy those who did. Now I see my struggles as having given me a deep appreciation of life, and of love, that I hope I succeed in passing on through the stories that I tell."

Dear Reader,

My life partner, Rob, is an adventurer. He knew how to
use a rifle before he knew how to spell Mississippi. I, on
the other hand, was raised with swimming lessons, story
time at the library and meat that came in nicely wrapped
packages from the grocery store. Because of having
Rob in my life I have found myself in places where it
is possible to be charged by a grizzly bear—and I was!
Quite frankly, I'm happier at home with a book, *but*
being thrown completely into an alien world, where I'm
uncomfortable, awkward and frightened, forces me to be
more than I was before.

This series, A FATHER'S WISH, begins with a delightful
what if. What if three young women, who had been
indulged their entire lives, were put in situations that
required more of them than had ever been required
before? Though my three heroines don't leave civilization
(though *they* might argue that point) the challenges they
face are grizzly bears to them! And, of course, they have
the most remarkable heroes to antagonize them, challenge
them, protect them and guide them.

I invite you to come with me as Brandy, Jessie and
Chelsea—one brave, one brainy, one beautiful—find out
life and love have plans for them that are beyond their
wildest dreams . . . .

Sincerely,

Cara Colter

Prologue

Two letters sat on his desk, both unopened, both marked *Personal and Confidential*. One was typed, the return address familiar to him. The second was addressed in handwriting, the feminine script of one not yet mature. He did not recognize that name or the return address. His hand hovered, and then he chose, hope and dread mixed within him.

Moments later, Winston Jacob King put down the typed letter and pinched the bridge of his nose between bony fingers. He felt shocked, all over again, though the letter only confirmed what his doctor had told him earlier in the week.

Dying.

He shouldn't be shocked. He was eighty-three years old. Had he really thought he was going to live forever?

The short answer? Yes.

Jake got up from behind his desk. A fire roared in the hearth, though it was a mild day. He was always cold, now.

He crossed the room, which was furnished in an eclectic mix of antiques. A thick Persian rug covered the aged oak floor, and Degas, Pissaro, Monet hung on the walls. But he noticed none of what it had taken him a lifetime to collect. Instead, he looked out the huge bay window.

His Southampton estate, Kingsway, lay before him. Tulips and daffodils splashed the spring beds with color. A gardener pruned the rosebushes. Beyond him were lush pastures and a Hanoverian mare, muscled and shiny, grazing contentedly while her foal frolicked.

The doctor had said he might have a year left, if they managed everything perfectly.

For some reason, as Jake looked out over his fields, a line from that haunting Johnny Cash song, played in his head.

"My empire of dirt," Jake murmured out loud. Once upon a time it had made him so proud that he—a man who had begun as a mechanic from the backwoods— had accomplished all this. In a recent issue of *Success Magazine*, Jake's company, Auto Kingdom, had been called the Costco of the automobile aficionado. Ridiculous, since he predated Costco by forty years.

Jake did not feel afraid of dying. No, what he felt was a sharp sense of sadness for his children, his three daughters. None were married, and he longed for the miracle of a grandchild.

"That's what you get for marrying so late in life," he berated himself. He'd been fifty-seven when his first daughter was born.

He went to the wall that was hung, window to window and ceiling to floor, with photographs of his princesses. His true treasures.

The wall documented the lives of his three daughters. Wasn't it just yesterday he had stood in front of the hospital, beaming so proudly, with Brandgwen, his first-born, in his arms? Wasn't it just a moment ago that Jessica had sat on that fat Welsh pony? Didn't only a breath separate him from the day he'd stood in the shadow of the Eiffel Tower with his baby Chelsea's small hand in his?

He felt such a rush of tenderness looking at their faces, the stamp of their personalities surviving the march of time. Brandy always looking faintly mischievous and lovely as a leprechaun, Jessica, looking studious, her green eyes huge behind those glasses, and his baby, Chelsea, twenty-two already, gorgeous and self-assured, always posing.

Brave, brainy and beautiful, his three daughters. Long ago, playing on his name and the American public's yearning for royalty, the press had dubbed his daughters princesses, and it had stuck for all these years.

The photographs showed lifestyles that might have been envied by real royalty. His throat ached as he looked at all his efforts to make them happy. The wall documented his daughters, at various ages, jumping their ponies, riding gondolas on the canals in Venice, skiing the slopes of the Alps. It documented the cars, the lavish birthday parties, the trinkets, the diamond tiaras, the gowns.

Oh, yes, Jake had gone into overdrive trying to insure the happiness of his daughters, after the scandalous death of his very young and very beautiful wife, more than twenty years ago.

There was no picture of Marcie on this wall. She had died when Brandy, their oldest daughter, had been six.

Brandy did not have her mother's looks—her face had always been impish rather than gorgeous. Dark sapphire-blue eyes were her only inheritance from her mother. She had hair as his own had once been—brown, thick, and just wavy enough to make it impossible to tame. Who knew where the freckles had come from? She had never outgrown them. She had been, to her mother's distress, happiest in overalls down at the stables. Brandy had a reckless streak in her, and it glittered in her eyes. The press had dubbed her the tomboy princess.

She was twenty-six, now, still as lithe as a young boy. And still a thrill seeker. Her bravery was legend. The King fortune had allowed her to pursue one adrenaline rush after another, and he had indulged her.

A mistake. Her latest "hobby" was BASE jumping. Her last jump had been from the top of the highest waterfall in the world, Angel Falls in Venezuela, every heart-stopping moment of it recorded by her faithful press. She'd always been like that, reckless.

But in light of his own news, he seemed to be seeing Brandy differently. She risked everything—except her heart.

Behind the dancing darkness of her eyes he could see the wariness in her.

Well, why wouldn't she be wary of love? She would have some memory of her mother's colossal indifference to her, the storminess of her parents' relationship.

He shifted his attention from Brandy to his other daughters, and with newfound depth, he felt the cruel weight of failure.

For all his efforts, were any of his princesses really happy? Not one of his daughters seemed to have a goal, a dream, a quest. Not one of them seemed to understand that love was everything.

Jessie, Jessica, his second daughter. She had hurtled through high school and entered university at seventeen. She was twenty-four now, and he had lost track of what degree she was working on. She talked of things he did not understand. Jessie seemed to be intellectual and disconnected. Despite having some kind of boyfriend—a fuddy-duddy professor who seemed about as exciting as day-old porridge—Jake saw heartbreaking loneliness in the lovely green of her astonishing eyes. Eyes hidden behind hideous glasses, and her gorgeous wheat-colored hair tucked into a prim bun that made her look like a spinster.

And then there was his baby, Chelsea. Ah, she was the darling of the press. Her picture was in some paper or magazine every time he went by a newsstand. She was the most like Marcie in looks, her beauty absolutely breathtaking. Her eyes were hazel, an exact mix of Marcie's blue and his own brown. Her hair floated nearly to her waist in a shiny wave of platinum blond. Her features were perfect, her mouth wide and generous.

She had her own staff—a hairstylist and a dresser who were so important to her she traveled with them. She kept such a high profile she had to have a bodyguard. Jake had indulged her, too, her every whim satisfied.

And yet he had the disconcerting feeling, when he was around Chelsea, that she wasn't able to see real beauty, that her world had become so superficial it had blinded her to what was real and good and genuine.

Jake kissed his fingertips and touched the images of his daughters' cheeks. His heart swelled within his chest, feeling as if it would break for loving them.

One year. Would that be enough to help his daughters discover what life was really all about? He wasn't going to play matchmaker. That would be disgraceful and manipulative.

But he had successfully created and run one of the largest corporations in the U.S. He knew that sometimes bringing the correct combination of people together, then leaving them alone, made remarkable and magical things happen.

Surely, a man who knew power as intimately as he did could do something so simple as set it up so his daughters could make the discovery that he himself had just made?

In the end, only one thing mattered.

Love.

Long ago, he had loved a woman, truly. She had not been like Marcie. She had not even been particularly pretty. But she had glowed with a genuine sweetness that, at the time, he had not fully appreciated. Lately, he awoke at night remembering the feeling of her head pressed into his neck, her dark hair scattered across his chest. He felt a sense of shattering loss now that he had not felt then.

Then, so busy building Auto Kingdom, so driven, that when she had talked to him of the future, of babies, he had been impatient. Perhaps he had even been cruel. Certainly insensitive, preoccupied with "important" matters.

He must have been, because she had gone away.

"Fiona," he called softly, and for a moment he could have sworn he felt her presence tingle across his spine, as warm and sweet as ever. It filled him with longing, which he impatiently brushed aside. He would not start acting old and feebleminded!

But he did realize that, save for his daughters, he might have missed love's glory all together. Was it too late to return to them the gift they had given him? If he could help them find love…

The shock lifted from him, the haze he had been walking in since opening the doctor's letter fell away. He became a man with a mission, a brilliant strategist who needed to get his most important affairs in order before he left this earth.

His most important affairs: Brandy, Jessie and Chelsea.

He returned to his desk. He would have to be crafty. He couldn't summon them all at once. They were smart girls, every one of them. Together they would sniff out a plot to meddle in their lives as easily as his hounds caught the scent of a fox.

No, he had to help them one at a time, and hope and pray that the clock wouldn't run out.

Aware that time was of the essence, he picked up the phone to his personal assistant. "James? Find Brandy. Get her home at once."

He picked up the letter and envelope from his doctor, crushed them in his hand, and moved to the fireplace. He hurtled them in.

Too late, he realized he had inadvertently crumpled the two letters—the one still unopened—together. He watched the girlish handwriting emerge from under the other burning paper, curl and then turn brown before it disappeared into flame.

A chill went up and down his spine, even though he could not know that he would have found the content of that second letter as devastating as that of the first….

Chapter One

"I do not love Clint McPherson," Brandy told herself tersely.

She had been repeating the phrase like a mantra since she'd left Kingsway, her father's home in Southampton on Long Island.

She was now driving, alone, on an unfamiliar road that twisted and wound around the shores of Lake of the Woods, a body of water so enormous that it was shared by two Canadian provinces and the state of Minnesota.

Finding one small cabin on it was beginning to look like an impossible task.

A cabin that belonged to none other than Clint McPherson.

Of course, she could say she hadn't been able to find it or him. End of mission. Who would really expect her to find a place on a map dotted with names like Minaki and Keewatin and Kenora? People who were under the illusion English was spoken in Canada should just have a look at this map!

What are you afraid of? an unwanted voice within her asked.

Brandgwen King had spent the majority of her life proving she was afraid of absolutely nothing, so the question irked. She was not afraid of Clint McPherson, or in love with him either! So, she'd had a girlhood crush on the man once. Big deal. It meant nothing. At twenty-six, she was all grown up now. The pain of how he had scorned her was long gone.

The point should be moot. The man in her life was Jason Morehead, her long time companion in adventure. Recently things had turned romantic, then unromantic, and now Jason was avidly begging her hand in marriage.

Why not marry him? He was wealthy, he was awesomely good-looking, he shared her taste for all things fast and furious.

"I don't love him," she said vehemently, and knew she was talking about Clint, even though she had been thinking of Jason, whom she was pretty sure she didn't love either. With pure frustration, Brandy pounded on the steering wheel of the red Ferrari she was driving.

Her father had arranged for her to have a car through a dealership connection in Winnipeg, Manitoba, where her flight from New York had landed several hours ago. She had been given the keys, told to use the car for as long as she needed it, no charge. It was a fact of life, in her circles, that the more money you had, the less you needed it.

Of course, that nice man had probably thought the

tomboy princess was going to be photographed in and around town in his car, not heading into some godforsaken wilderness.

"Love Clint McPherson?" she said out loud, with a derisive snort. "More like hate him."

How had she gotten back to that when she'd been thinking, with determination, about the nice man who had lent her the nice car?

She sighed, annoyed with herself, and then surrendered. Hate? That seemed a bit strong for a man she had not seen for nearly seven years, not since he'd totally spoiled her nineteenth birthday party.

"Indifferent," she decided, and then announced it out loud, putting down her window and calling it to the giant fir trees that lined the road. "I am indifferent to Clint McPherson."

It rang of a lie. She knew it. The trees probably knew it, too. She put her window back up, took a twist in the road a trifle too quickly and slowed marginally.

How could her father have asked this of her? And why had she said yes?

She thought back to her meeting with her father, and the frown of concentration deepened on her face.

He had seemed old.

Of course, he was old. He'd always been old, even when she was young!

But he had never *seemed* old.

She was coming to see Clint because her father had asked her to. And maybe because she needed time to sort through all the implications of Jason's unexpected announcement of his deep and undying love.

It was that simple. She had not agreed to this trip because she harbored some secret wish to see Clint again. She had come because her father asked things of her so rarely. He didn't know it, but if he ever said to her that he wished she would not do some of the things that she did—like jumping out of airplanes or, more recently, off cliffs, buildings and bridges—then she would stop, just like that, no questions asked.

But he never asked.

Now he had asked something. He was old, yes, but beloved to her. The truth was Brandy would do anything for him, this gentle man who had loved her, and her sisters, so unconditionally, forever.

She thought back on the conversation she'd had with him. She had been distracted by the heat in the room, the fire blazing, so his request had really caught her up the side of the head.

"Brandy," he'd said. "I need a favor. Clint—"

Her heart had done that traitorous flip-flop at the sound of his name.

"—has not recovered from Rebecca's death."

Rebecca, the woman Clint McPherson had married, was a woman who had been everything Brandy was not. Because Rebecca was a lawyer for Jake's company, Brandy had known her slightly, well enough to know she was composed, classy, refined. Her hair was of the tameable variety, her makeup never ran and her clothing never rumpled.

Brandy's chestnut locks, on the other hand, had a will of their own. Her style depended largely on humidity, direction of the wind and other forces beyond her control. Even when she tried to tame her masses of wavy hair, a few tresses always defiantly sprang free, giving her an impish look that went well with the nickname *tomboy princess* the press had given her long ago, and that she had never managed to outgrow.

Added to that, she had never learned the subtleties of proper makeup application, despite her younger sister Chelsea's many efforts to show her.

And clothing? She relied heavily on many-pocketed cargo pants and T-shirts. To Chelsea's horror, sweats were her sister's favorite fashion statement.

Brandy knew her lack of fashion acumen was a disappointment to the American public who had long ago made Jake King's motherless daughters into *their* princesses. At least she had not opted out of the role entirely, like her sister Jessie. No, Brandy tried never to disappoint in the fast-living department. Not parties or drugs, no, just lots of rich-kid fun: big engines, fast horses, white water. She had discovered the love of her life when she was sixteen and had sky-dived for the first time. The new thrill was BASE jumping.

Her lack of ability to make a stunning personal fashion statement was part of the reason she had not attended Clint's wedding, though she had been invited, of course. Clint was like family, her father's right-hand man since Brandy had been fourteen.

Younger, and so much more dynamic than the rest of that inner circle, Clint had fairly bristled with a kind of dangerous energy that had made her skin tingle.

"Back when I was young and hopelessly naive," she

told herself, taking a curve much too quickly. Clint would not make her skin tingle, now.

Good grief, no. She hung out with Jason Morehead, *People* magazine's number-two pick as the world's sexiest and most eligible bachelor.

Still, Brandy had made sure she was a world away the day Clint McPherson had spoiled her fondest fantasy by marrying someone else. She had sent a lavish gift—a complete set of antique silverware—if she recalled. On the day Clint had said, "I do," Brandy had been paddling frantically through the foaming, freezing waters in the Five Finger Rapids section of the Yukon River.

And for the birth of Clint and Rebecca's daughter—the same. An exquisite, expensive gift—a handmade bassinet from Italy—but Brandy had been a no-show at the christening party. She'd been arrested for jumping off the New River Gorge Bridge in Virginia for the utterly ridiculous reason that it wasn't "Bridge Day," the only day of the year that BASE jumping was legal off the 876-foot height.

And then, shockingly, only days after the christening, Rebecca had died. Brandy had known, because of Clint's longstanding relationship with her family, that she'd had to go to the funeral. But somehow she had ended up at Angel Falls in Venezuela instead. She'd sent a card and an extravagant, tasteful, subdued spray of white roses.

"It's been more than a year," her father had said, sadly. "He does some work from home, but he's become reclusive. He stays at that cabin in Canada, with a baby, and when I talk to him he seems so detached, unnaturally cool, as if nothing touches him."

Brandy had listened to her father, and thought, a bit cynically, that there was nothing new about Clint being detached or unnaturally cool. But her heart insisted on hearing the words her father didn't say. Clint had loved Rebecca so much that he planned to mourn forever.

"Brandy, I want you to go to him."

It was probably been the heat in the room, but for a moment she actually thought she was going to faint. "What?" she stammered.

"You were always the one who could make him laugh. Go and make Clint laugh again."

"I don't recall making him laugh," she said stiffly. "I recall making him very, very angry on several occasions."

"Precisely," her father said with satisfaction.

"Sorry?"

"Brandy, you make him feel strongly. Go there. Make him laugh, or make him angry, but make him feel *something*."

The room was silent for a long time while she pondered what he was asking of her. She gave him the only possible answer.

"I can't," she said softly. "Really. I can't."

Then her father did something he had never done before.

He covered her hand with his, and she felt the tremble in it. His eyes locked on hers, and she saw the weariness there and the pleading. Then he whispered, "Please."

She stared at him and heard his desperation, heard that he was begging her to do this thing for him.

She felt the shock of it, knew the depth of his love for the man who had stood so loyally at his side for so long, and knew she could not refuse her father this request, even if it threatened the most secret places within her, even if she knew it was absurd to put herself in this position.

She was not going to be able to rescue Clint.

Still, her father's hand trembling on top of hers and the stifling heat in the room and the desperation in his voice had made her say yes, she would go there. She would try.

Besides, it would give her a week or two to figure out what to do about Jason.

So now, pretty sure she was lost in the Canadian wilds, she stopped once again and studied her instructions. She was in the heart of lake country now. Down the occasional long, winding driveway, she caught a glimpse of a posh resort, a private cabin, heavenly worlds that promised the perfect summer. But it was still early in the year, spring, and the countryside seemed largely abandoned.

"I do not love Clint McPherson," she told herself, and gave herself a shake, wondering how her thoughts had gone there when she had been focusing so fiercely on the spring landscapes around her.

She put the car back in gear and took the next series of twists in the road fast enough to make her heart hammer within her throat.

That was how she always handled emotion. She shoved it away with adrenaline.

"My drug of choice," she muttered. She thought it was a fairly good one, too. Much better than booze or drugs or food, or the worst one of all, men.

She slammed on the brakes, put the car in reverse.

A small copper sign, mounted on a tasteful stone post, glinted in the sun, nearly lost among the thick green foliage that surrounded it. It marked a private driveway.

Touch the Flame.

She was here then. She took a deep breath and recognized she was afraid. So she did what she always did when she felt that uncomfortable little fissure of fear.

She put the gas pedal down so hard that she was sucked back into her seat as if she were on a launch.

The car rocketed up a scenic lane, lined on both sides with gigantic fir trees. The road climbed a gentle rise, and she slammed on the brakes again at the top, her breath caught in her throat.

She had seen some of the most beautiful places on earth.

Yet this place caught at her heart. The road curved downward, opening suddenly out of woods into a beautiful clearing.

It wasn't exactly a cabin that stood there, but a log house, golden, sweeping, windows everywhere. It was on the edge of a manicured lawn that swept downward to the sparkling gray-blue lake waters. The property was located on a sheltered bay, completely private, natural rocks standing like powerful sentinels at the mouth of the cove. Beds of flowers rimmed the lawns, looking wild and glorious. It did not look like the property of a man who was living in misery.

It occurred to her, within minutes, she would see him again. Her heart beating in her throat, she drove slowly down to the house. She parked her vehicle beside a carport that held a silver Escalade.

She got out of her car and shut the door quietly. The fragrance of the trees wrapped around her, clean and pure, heaven-scented. At first she thought it was silent, almost eerily so, but then she could hear the call of birds, the insulted chatter of a squirrel, the lap of the water on the nearby shore.

Had she expected Clint to come out and greet her? Perhaps he had not heard her arrive. There was still time for her to get back in that car, ease her way back out that long driveway, *save herself.*

"Save myself," she muttered. "Sheesh."

She took a deep breath and walked around the front of the house on a beautiful black flagstone pathway that curved around and then spilled into a huge patio, of the same stone, that ran the entire length of the house. The front was even more impressive than the back. Outside living was obviously the priority here, a wide-timbered staircase led to a multitiered deck. On the first tier was a hot tub, on the second, lounge chairs with thick, colorful, yellow-striped cushions. Outside the French-paned doors leading into the house were a stainless-steel barbecue, a bright yellow umbrella table and matching cushioned chairs. Buckets of flowers were everywhere.

Then she spotted a lone pink bunny, and it seemed sadly out of place among all the sophisticated deck furnishings.

She turned away from the house, shaded her eyes against the brilliance of the sun glinting off the water, and scanned the yard.

A movement in the deep shadows in the farthest corner of the green grass caught her eye and stopped her heart.

Him.

Clint McPherson in the flesh.

Apparently he had not heard her arrival. He was in shorts, crouched over one of the flower beds, a spade in one hand, a bedding plant in the other.

If part of her had hoped that age had been cruel to him, that part of her was thwarted. Even from here she could see the power of his build, the grace and ease of his movement. He was wearing crisp khaki shorts and a navy-blue sports shirt. She could see the muscular line of his legs, the broad sweep of his shoulders, the muscles in his forearms leap and cord with each minute movement.

His hair was longer than she ever remembered it being, touching the collar of his short-sleeved shirt.

But she remembered that hair, thick and wavy, its color a burnished bronze that turned to spun gold in the sun.

The hair had always made her think of him as a throwback to some ancient and fierce Scottish warrior. For even in his business attire—knife-creased pants; white, starched shirt; conservative tie; black, polished shoes—even then, she had always seen that he was not what the rest of them were.

It was not just that he was not flabby or soft; it was that, in the most subtle of ways, he was not completely civilized. There was a look in his eyes of a man who had seen things, felt things, been at the center of things, that were hard and crude, perhaps even cruel. He had carried himself, back then, with the unconscious grace of a predator, alert, powerful, guarded.

He straightened suddenly, and she knew that part of him was unchanged—his instinct had warned him he was no longer alone. He stood and swung around, and Brandy saw the familiar grace and power in every line of his magnificent body.

Her breath caught in her throat and her foolish heart beat too fast.

His face was a study in unrelenting masculine angles. He had a strong nose, pronounced cheekbones; the line of his jawbone was straight and true. His chin, shadowed faintly with whiskers that were bronze tipped, hinted at a cleft. His lips were firm and sensuous.

His eyes were the tawny gold of a lion's eyes, and every bit as watchful, every bit as *ready,* as they swept his property now.

She sensed two things immediately.

Her father had been right. Something was wrong. Despite the look of ordered perfection around the lake house, the light that had always flared in those eyes, brilliant and fierce, had an element in it she did not understand. It was as if ice and fire battled within him, and ice was winning.

The second thing she sensed and could not ignore was that her skin was tingling treacherously. She knew that she had wasted her time chanting her mantra all the way here. She loved Clint McPherson in some fierce and primal way she was not sure she could ever tame.

Nonsense, she told herself. *Utter hogwash.*

She drew in a deep breath and reprimanded herself firmly for her moment of weakness. She had been taming the untamable her whole life!

She was here on assignment for her father. Her assignment was to bring back the Clint they knew.

But regarding him now, across the space of his well-manicured yard, she wondered if anyone had ever known him—or ever would.

But she had a third realization. She was also on assignment for herself.

Get over it, once and for all. It was probably this silly infatuation with Clint that was preventing her from jumping at Jason's proposal.

She would lay her childish heartbreaks and hopes to rest. She would see Clint McPherson through the realistic eyes of a mature woman and tame that thing inside of her that *wanted* him.

Her exact words on her nineteenth birthday, if she recalled, and of course she did, in every excruciating and humiliating detail.

He looked at her for a long time, his expression unreadable, but certainly in no way welcoming. There was an impenetrable shield in his eyes, and his lips remained in a firm line. He folded his arms over the expanse of his chest, formidable, the lines of his face and body totally uninviting. Yet for all the rugged barriers set up by his body language, the unyielding expression on his face, the question that crowded her mind was *How could a man approaching forty look so damned good?*

Well, all you had to do was look at the men in Hollywood: Harrison, Tom, the other Clint. Some men aged well, like wine, and he was one of them.

Unfortunately.

She forced herself to move forward. She was good at this—looking over the side of a cliff or off the edge of the fiftieth floor of a skyscraper—and grinning with reckless abandon, as if nothing mattered to her, as if she knew no fear.

She strode toward him. "Hey," she said. "Sober-sides! Long time, no see."

He inclined his head toward her, acknowledgment; his eyes narrowed, no smile. Not that she had expected one. He hated being called Sober-sides almost as much as she hated being called Brandgwen.

Before they could really take up their battle stations, the shrubs parted beside him and a gurgle emerged, followed by a baby, on all fours, her face dirty, her diaper swollen.

Brandy slowed her advance, entranced. Thirteen months. She knew the baby's age, exactly.

Clint's focus had shifted to his baby, too. That hard light in his eyes and the grim lines of his face softened, and for the briefest moment she caught sight of a vulnerability so immense it shook her to her core. But his face closed again, almost instantly, and she looked quickly away, almost terrified by the fact she might have glimpsed tenderness in him.

It seemed to be a good strategy, given the insanely wild beating of her heart. Brandy got down on her knees before his daughter.

The child was beautiful, her eyes the same tawny color as his, her shoulder-length hair a riot of messy red curls, freckles spattered across her fair skin. She put her thumb in her mouth and drew enthusiastically on it, her eyes narrowed.

Brandy glanced from the father to the daughter.

They were eyeing her with identical expressions of wariness, as if an enemy had trespassed the sanctuary of the clan camp.

"Brandgwen."

She winced when he said her name, and at first he thought it was the gravel in his voice, but then he remembered she hated that form of her name. She preferred Brandy. Well, that was okay. He preferred almost anything to Sober-sides. A simple thing—the exchange of greetings—and yet already he could feel the friction between them.

He had not seen her for a long time, and he felt the shock of her presence, the subtle electricity of her. Of course, he had seen her in photographs, more recently in newspapers and magazines that could not seem to get enough of the oldest and youngest King girls. Just last month, he had caught a glimpse of her on the evening news after she had performed another outrageous stunt.

The cameras had caught the wild tangle of her hair, the devil-may-care quality of her grin, the jauntiness of her wave.

But had missed—as every photo and film sequence seemed to miss—her astounding essence.

Brandy King was not a pretty girl. Her features were too strong, much like her father's, and the cameras had an almost cruel capacity to capture her lack of traditional beauty. Photographed, she always managed to look intensely ordinary, a plain Jane with an attitude. She also played down her absolutely stunning curves by dressing like a boy.

Photographs, even interviews on television, always totally failed to capture her fire, that mysterious *something* that was extraordinarily sensual and compelling.

Up close and personal, it was a different story. Her eyes, as sapphire as that lake when it changed color at dawn, glittered with that inner spark, an unsettling combination of mischief and passion. Her hair was dark and thick and shiny. It didn't look as if she had run a comb through it anytime today, and when she saw him looking at it, she registered his look as disapproval, and tossed her hair with the spirited defiance of a wild horse tossing her mane. That grin was reckless and devil-may-care and totally disarming.

The simple truth was that Brandgwen King meant trouble.

She always had.

Yet when her father, Jake, had called and asked if she could stay with Clint and Becky at the lake for a little while, how could he refuse?

Jake was more than a business associate, more than his boss. He was Clint's friend, his mentor, the closest thing he had ever had to a father. Jake had once seen something in a rough kid from the wrong side of the tracks and had believed in that something until it had come true.

Jake had offered no explanation for the imminent arrival of his eldest daughter, but Clint had assumed Brandy's penchant for adventure mixed with mischief had left her in some kind of mess and that she needed to hide out until it blew over.

Well, there was no hideout quite like this one.

He'd been hiding successfully from the pain in his life for over a year and planned to keep on doing so.

He felt a small hand on his leg, and his daughter pulled herself to standing, swung behind his leg and then peeped out at Brandy with caution and reserve. Her diaper drooped nearly to her knees and her face showed telltale signs she had been sampling the dirt—again.

That feeling of inadequacy swept over him. He was a man accustomed to being in charge, but being entrusted with the care of his infant daughter had thrown him into an entirely different arena. He was like a man in a foreign land, lost, uncertain of which direction to take, having no grasp for the new language of his new world. He was fighting, as was his instinct, not to let it show that with his tiny daughter he came face-to-face with his own weaknesses and uncertainties every day.

But he was a disciplined man, and so he was careful not to let any of this slip onto his features. Brandy had a gift for sniffing out weakness and exploiting it. On her nineteenth birthday, just a little bit tipsy, hadn't she seen his greatest weakness?

"So, you're a shy one, are you?" Brandy said, still at Becky's level, crouched easily on her haunches, her voice a rich imitation of a brogue.

The baby shrank even farther behind his knee.

Without warning, Brandy grabbed his other knee, ducked behind it, and peeped out at his daughter.

He felt shocked by her touch, the fire in her fingertips where they bit into the flesh below his knee. There was no mistaking, even from this brief encounter, that the oldest of the Misses King was not a child anymore.

And she had been a most dangerous child. How much more dangerous would she be as a full-grown, full-blooded woman?

He gazed down at her, the thick, rippling richness of the dark hair cascading over slender shoulders, the swell of her breasts under the thin fabric of a black tank top held up on the whim of two tiny little straps. She was wearing low-slung sweatpants that rode a little too low with her crouched like that and that clung to the delectable curves of her athletic legs.

She stuck out her tongue at his daughter, crossed her eyes.

Becky tried valiantly to make herself invisible, but not before he caught a ghost of a smile tickle her lips.

"Excuse me," he said, inserting enough ice to sink the *Titanic* into his voice. "Would you mind letting go of my leg?"

"Becky," Brandy said sternly, "you heard the man. Let go of your father's leg."

His little girl's eyes went very round and she let go instantly.

"I meant you!" He scooped up Becky, and she buried her face in his chest.

"Oh," Brandy said innocently, but thankfully, she unhanded his leg, rose easily, and stuck out her hand. Her eyes danced with amusement.

"Of course you meant me, Sober-sides. How are you?"

He shifted the minuscule weight of the baby from the crook of his right arm to his left and took Brandy's proffered hand with a certain reluctance. He felt the heat and unexpected strength of her grasp, and let it go instantly.

"Fine, thank you," he said, his tone clipped.

"A conversationalist as always," she said. "Becky, how on earth are you learning to talk around this man of many words?"

How had she managed to hit such a sensitive spot after only seconds of being here? Was his daughter supposed to be talking more than she was? At just over a year, she had mastered *da-da* and *poo-poo*. That was it. The whole vocabulary.

"I thought I'd put you in the cottage," he said abruptly. "It's private."

The thought of having her under the very same roof was a little more than he could handle.

Aware that the diaper was definitely a little far gone, Clint led the way across the clearing and down a small stone path with as much dignity as he could given that something warm and wet was leaking onto his arm. At the end of the path was a small guest cottage.

"It's adorable," Brandy said with genuine enthusiasm, as if she didn't have an upscale apartment in New York and a house in Bel Air, as if she hadn't stayed in palaces and five-star hotels all over the world. "Does it come with seven little men? And a prince?"

Seven men and a prince. He'd known she had become a dangerous woman.

"No," he said tersely. "No men, no prince, no maids, no cook, no dishwasher, not a single amenity that you are used to."

His voice crackled with unfriendliness.

Which, naturally, Brandy did not hear or chose not to hear.

"You have no idea what I'm used to," she said cheerfully. "I slept with bugs as big as my fist in Brazil."

"I remember you used to be scared of bugs," he said, then could have kicked himself at the memory he had just conjured. Brandy, fourteen, in a much-too-skimpy bathing suit by the pool, standing on one of the deck chairs, pointing at some huge black insect that had crawled out of the filtration system.

He'd done the gentlemanly thing, dispatched the bug. When it had looked like she planned to leap into his arms in gratitude, he'd told her, coldly, her bathing suit was inappropriate.

But the part he remembered the most clearly was not the bathing suit or the bug. It was her saying softly, "Don't tell anyone I was scared. Please."

From that moment on, it was as though he knew a secret about her, a secret that made the heart he wasn't supposed to have ache every time she did one more foolhardy or death-defying stunt.

Had she really conquered that long-ago fear of bugs? He didn't want to know. He didn't want to know one single thing about her.

Except what her lips tasted like.

"You must be very tired," he said, abruptly, damning her silently for how little had changed between them. "You've come a long way today."

"I'm never tired," Brandy said.

Of course not. She was a woman who would have

you believe she could handle seven men and a prince and anything else life threw at her, including bugs as big as her fist. Only, looking at her, he saw something flicker in her eyes, and wondered how much of it was all a front. He cut off that line of thought before it made her even more dangerous than she already was—which was plenty dangerous.

"Did you want me to bring your things from the car?"

She tossed him the keys, her expectation of being waited on as unconscious to her as breathing. She went up the cottage steps two at a time and burst in. Somehow he didn't want to see her gushing over the cuteness of the accommodations. Still hefting the soggy Becky on his arm, he went up to the parking area behind the house.

A Ferrari, no less, and crammed floor to roof with her things as if she were thinking of staying for a long, long while. He counted three full-size suitcases and two overnight bags. There were several dresses hung in bags. There was a tennis racket, a riding helmet and a new blow-up dinghy that hadn't been taken out of the box.

He didn't have a tennis court or horses. There was no place, that he was aware of, within a hundred miles where a woman could wear dresses like that. The lake water wouldn't be warm enough for weeks yet to risk capsizing her floating device in it.

Resigned, he set the baby on her padded rear and kept one eye on whether or not she was trying to ingest rocks while he began unloading Brandy's vehicle.

"She'll be bored in ten minutes," he reassured himself as the pile of her belongings became a small mountain on the ground beside him.

So, she'd get bored, and then she would leave.

"She'll last two days," he bet himself, and felt his black mood lift slightly. "Three at the outside."

"Poo-poo," the baby commented, but he couldn't tell if she was agreeing with him, or if she was "pooh-poohing" him. She was a female after all, and even a pint-sized member of the fairer sex was probably blessed with intuition. Perhaps his wee daughter sensed that the thing he was worst at—besides choosing girl clothes for a one-year-old—was predicting how anything was going to go once Brandy King was in the vicinity.

Chapter Two

It was the dawn of day four, and Brandy King was still happily ensconced in his little guesthouse.

"I'm losing my touch," Clint decided. The baby was still asleep, and he usually enjoyed these quiet moments before she awakened, sipping his coffee, planning his day, enjoying his garden.

The love of gardening was a bit of a surprise. His father would have turned over in his grave to see his eldest son so content with dirt on his hands, and flower gardens growing around him. Clint himself had been unable to decipher the pull of it.

But this morning he looked out his kitchen window to the back of his property, not to his gardens in the front. No, he was focused on where her red Ferrari was still parked and he was aware his jaw hurt, as if he had been clenching it in his sleep, not surprising given the tension his houseguest made him feel.

Every morning, he got up hoping that car would be gone, hoping that some time in the night it would have occurred to her how bored she was and she would have left.

He had predicted two days—three—at the very outside, and he'd been wrong.

The thing was he was rarely wrong about human nature. That was the strength he gave Jake and Auto Kingdom; that was the skill behind his meteoric rise in the company.

A tumultuous childhood, filled with the rage and pain of his parents, had given Clint a rare and valuable gift. At the time, he had not recognized it as a gift. His ability to look at a person and judge instantly whether they were a friend or a foe, to be able to feel with one-hundred-percent accuracy the mood in a room, to be able to read the truth in a person's eyes, no matter what their lips were saying, had been a survival tool.

That survival tool had been one in an arsenal of survival skills that had kept him and his younger brother, Cameron, out of harm's way. That usually meant his father's foul temper and fists, but they had both grown to manhood in a mean neighborhood where book-learning was scorned and street smarts were everything. Clint knew how to use his mind, and he knew how to use his fists, and he grew up using them both with regularity.

He would have never guessed it would be the unerring instinct about people, rather than his ability with his fists, that would decide his future. But Jake King had spotted him in a group of young apprentices working at one of Auto Kingdom's tire shops, talked to him for a few minutes, and his destiny had changed. He had moved, at first uncomfortably, into a world where he had been certain he did not belong. It had not taken him long to figure out that, under the masks, most men were the same. And that became his job. To unmask men.

"What's your measure of that man, Clint?" Jake would ask at some high-level meeting.

Clint could always tell. The light in the man's eyes, the way he stood, the way he interacted with others, the grip of his handshake. Inevitably, Clint found himself at more and more meetings, more and more a part of the Auto Kingdom decision-making process, more and more part of the inner circle, more and more Jake's right-hand man.

But now, taking another sip of his coffee and balefully eyeing the red Ferrari, he admitted he was losing his touch, not that "the touch" had ever been applicable to Brandy. Reading her would be like trying to read the wind. She was elusive and mysterious, one minute all woman, the next a wonder-filled child.

He had read wrong, been sure she would have been gone by now. But, if she was bored, she was pretending not to be, though sniffing out subterfuge was usually one of his specialities. She liked the baby and seemed to have a genuine way with her, which surprised him. He would not have put Brandy and a baby together in an equation that worked. But then who was Brandy, really? Did anyone know? Since her arrival, she always seemed to be full of laughter and mischief, as if life itself entertained her even when there were no tall buildings to leap off.

"One more day," he said. He hoped so. Not that he didn't appreciate her interest in Becky, but Brandy was disruptive without half trying. She didn't cook and she didn't pick up after herself. She walked around in boyish outfits that had never been meant to contain feminine curves and that were strangely alluring because of that.

He was ever conscious she was his boss's daughter, off-limits for that reason alone, though if he wanted more reasons, he could find them. She was too young for him. She was frivolous. Though he and Jake had never discussed it, Jake probably expected his daughters to marry into the social circle he had spent his life earning his way into. It was one that Clint, for all he had won Jake's respect and loyalty, did not fit into mostly because he lacked any desire to be a part of those worlds of pure wealth and power.

Still, Brandy did make Clint's solemn little girl laugh, but what kind of price was he willing to pay for that?

His own peace of mind was in jeopardy—his aching jaw was a constant reminder of that—and he prized his peace of mind more highly than anything.

It was hard to be around a woman who was so vital and alive without feeling these uncomfortable, and totally inappropriate, stirrings of awareness.

Without remembering, dammit, what her lips had tasted like all those years ago.

She had forced him into trying to be invisible on his own property. He felt like the man servant, Jeeves, looking after her but trying to be unobtrusive about it. Trying to maintain his own space and sanity, while she tried to tease him out of it.

He hadn't tested Brandy's love of Becky as far as a diaper change. He brightened, a man with a plan. If she showed no sign of going, he'd ask her to handle one of those. Poo-poo with any luck. That should have the princess packing her car and driving back up that road….

Clint heard a deep rumbling, and frowned. A large vehicle was obviously laboring up the other side of the rise, and he turned his attention to his road.

Sure enough, an enormous truck—a moving van from the logo on the side—lurched over the crest of the hill, geared down noisily and began its descent into his backyard.

A moving van?

Had he misread the situation that badly? Not only was Brandy not leaving, but she was settling in more permanently?

"God give me strength," Clint muttered, taking his coffee cup and going out the back screen door to meet the truck.

It had pulled to a halt in the parking area, which was not designed for trucks.

A redheaded kid with a pack of cigarettes stuck in the arm of his T-shirt rolled down the window and grinned at him.

"Wow," he said. "That's a hell of a trip for a tramp."

A tramp? Clint felt relief wash over him. He wasn't quite sure what the kid meant by a tramp, but obviously he was at the wrong address, an easy enough mistake to make along the lake roads.

"You have the wrong place," he said.

"Brandy King's house, right?"

Fury, red-hot, boiled up in Clint. Okay, she was reckless and a brat and annoying as all get out, but nobody was calling her a tramp in his presence. He wasn't the least bit happy that his first impulse was to open that door, yank the kid out, and plow a fist into his face. He'd always known that part of himself, the fighter, was only buried, not banished.

But before he got to step one, he heard a cheery hello called out and turned to see Brandy coming around the corner of the house. She looked like she had just tumbled from bed, her hair springing around her head, uncombed, her clothing rumpled, her feet bare.

Unless Clint was mistaken, which was possible given his record of the last few days, she was wearing her pajamas, a pair of bright yellow low-slung pants with a drawstring waist and a skimpy narrow-strapped top that didn't quite cover her belly button.

Which was pierced.

The morning air was chill, and her nipples were hard against the thin fabric of the top.

"God in heaven have mercy," Clint muttered.

The young deliveryman said, "You're not kidding."

Clint's hands formed fists at his sides and the fury deepened within him, especially when he turned back to the driver and saw the look of lascivious male interest on his face as Brandy sashayed toward them.

The younger man's eyes met his, and apparently the

street fighter Clint had once been was riding pretty close to the surface because suddenly the truck driver was examining his bill of lading instead of Brandy.

"Another gorgeous morning," she said, arriving at the truck, completely unaware of the explosive tension in the air.

"Maybe you should go get a sweater," Clint said tersely.

She looked momentarily puzzled, then caught on. She flashed him a careless grin and then folded her arms over her chest.

He cursed under his breath, took the bill of lading that the truck driver handed him and signed it without looking.

This is exactly what he'd always disliked about Brandy. He knew control was essential to life, to survival, and yet around her, he never quite knew what was going to happen next, or worse, how he was going to react to it.

"Please tell me you aren't moving here," he said, and he saw the hurt look before she carefully masked it.

"Sober-sides! You mean you aren't enjoying my company?"

"If he isn't, I will," the young driver said hopefully, and then ducked his head at the killing look Clint gave him.

"Aren't you the sweetest thing?" Brandy gushed, making Clint unsure which of them he wanted to kill first.

She thought the kid was sweet, the kid thought she was a tramp. Hadn't she learned anything about the real world from all the years she had spent gallivanting around it?

That was the problem. He was a man who had learned to fight as naturally as he had learned to breathe. And that part of him had never been completely laid to rest, though it was buried under layers of refinement, education, wealth.

But Brandy brought his primal, rough instinct so quickly to the surface it was as if it had never been tamed at all.

He slid her a look. It would be impossible to call her beautiful and yet she was an undeniable presence. Electricity and pure energy seemed to crackle in the air around her. The young driver was acting like a fly caught in her web.

"Have you got something to unload?" Clint snapped.

"Oh, yeah. The tramp."

"Maybe you better explain to me what you mean by that," Clint ordered edgily, sliding Brandy a look to make sure her bosom was still covered.

"The trampoline. I'm to deliver it and put it together. Where did you want it?"

"A trampoline," Clint repeated, stunned. All that fury and protectiveness wasted on a misinterpretation? He didn't misinterpret things. He really was losing his touch, and it was her fault. He turned to Brandy. "A trampoline?" he demanded, as if the driver had said he was unloading an order of M-16s instead of a child's toy.

"I got one for Becky," Brandy told him, inordinately pleased with herself.

"Could I see you for a minute?"

He took her elbow and took her out of earshot of the young man who was a little too avidly interested in her.

"Do you think maybe you could have asked me before you went to all this trouble?" he asked.

"Oh! It hasn't been any trouble. I mean it has been,

because you should see what you have to go through to get a trampoline to the way-back-beyond, but it was kind of fun and I didn't have anything better to do."

"I don't want Becky to have a trampoline," he said, with all the firmness he could muster, given that the scent of her was wrapping itself around him, as sweet as sunshine on lavender, and nearly as drugging.

"You don't want her to have one?" she exclaimed, as if he were an ogre who lived under a bridge. "You can't mean that!"

"They are extremely dangerous toys. Do you know how many serious injuries are caused by trampolines every year?"

"No," she said, tossing her hair defiantly, "but why am I not surprised you would have those statistics at your fingertips?"

"She's barely pulling herself to standing. She does not need a trampoline!"

"Oh, Clint, let her have it, for God's sake. We'll be careful. I promise. You can make all kinds of rules around it. She'll never be on it by herself, ever. I won't do anything dangerous. I promise. No flips, or anything like that."

"You aren't happy with just trying to break your own neck all the time? You have to try and break my daughter's?"

"Clint! The poor child should be walking, shouldn't she? It will help her strengthen her legs. Besides, she hardly ever laughs. You guys need my help around here."

She was hitting him in his sensitive spots now.

Should Becky be walking? He didn't know these things, and the family doctor told him not to worry, but he worried. Should she be laughing more? Was she missing everything it was to be a child because she was stuck here with a man who knew so little about children? Once, he had thought fierce love should be enough. Now, he wasn't so sure. Maybe his daughter did need a trampoline.

Brandy sensed him weakening, which was a bad thing. He put on his sternest expression. "You want to be a help around here?"

She nodded solemnly.

"Well, every single day meals have to get put on the table. Laundry has to get done. There's more to having a baby around than entertaining her. In case you haven't noticed—"

He felt her hand on his arm, which was nearly as disconcerting as the scent of her and her nipples showing through her camisole.

"Could we just talk about the trampoline for now? Can we keep it? Please?" she said. "I'll accept responsibility for it."

"That would be a first," he said.

She laughed and kissed him on the cheek as if he were some dotty old uncle that she favored.

He was surprised at the level of offense he felt at her apparent relegation of him to a platonic position. He was surprised by how the touch of her lips made him feel anything but platonic. He was surprised by how a perfectly normal morning could be turned absolutely topsy-turvy in the blink of an eye.

Especially if that eye was the color of lake water at twilight.

"I knew you'd say yes," she said. "And I promise I'll help with other things."

Had he said yes? The touch of her lips, feather soft, on his cheek had him feeling confused. He had the awful feeling he'd opened the doors to a three-ring circus.

Laughing, she raced back to the truck, forgetting to cover herself, and the next thing he knew, her and the kid were unloading the trampoline—which was enormous and ugly—and picking out a place on his beloved grass for it.

The kid was gazing at Brandy with a look on his face that Clint didn't like one little bit.

He managed to insert himself between the two of them. He took over supervising the assembly of the trampoline. Apparently his body language to the young driver, who had managed to tell her his name was Frankie, had been ineffective.

He really was losing his touch!

Brandy walked Frankie back to his truck once the trampoline—big, black and blue, and not at all in keeping with Clint's landscaping plan—was sitting dead center on the front lawn.

"Thank you so much for bringing it all the way out here," she told him, just as if she hadn't paid a king's ransom for the delivery.

Unfortunately, her friendliness was a little too encouraging.

"Th-th-there's a movie—" he started, shot Clint a look and stopped, blushing.

Brandy laughed. "You are sweet. A movie?"

"No," Clint snapped. "No movie. That's all, Frank. If you're done here, you can leave."

The young driver sent her a look, but thankfully bowed to the authority he heard in Clint's voice.

"Yessir," he said glumly.

Which made Clint feel about a hundred years older than him—and her—which he was.

He turned back to Brandy after watching the truck back out of the parking spot, turn around and head back up the drive.

She still had her hands folded and was tapping her foot.

He recognized the mutinous expression on her face from her childhood, only she wasn't a child anymore.

"You were rude," she said. "He was just being nice."

So, he, who had the good sense to protect her, was rude. But the kid was nice.

"Whatever," he said, folding his arms over his chest and eyeing her narrowly.

"If I want to go to a movie with him, I will," she said grimly.

"Not while you're here you won't."

"Clint! I am not a teenager anymore."

"Well, then try acting like a responsible adult."

"Excuse me?"

"You are one of the wealthiest young women on the continent. You can't just go to the movies with a kid who drives up in a truck. You know nothing about him."

"He didn't know anything about me, either!"

Clint snorted.

"Sometimes I have trouble deciphering exactly what your disapproving grunts mean," she said icily.

"Okay. Let me spell it out for you. Unless Frankie is a monk, which—" from the way his eyes had been glued to her nipples, he wasn't "—which I highly doubt, he knew exactly who you were. You gave him your real name for the delivery. You've been the darling of the press since you were a tot, Princess Tomboy, and you still manage to get your face and name splashed in the headlines fairly frequently."

"I think he liked me for me," she said stubbornly.

Clint ignored the hope he heard in her voice. "Well, that just goes to show you are still incredibly naive."

"Plus, he was cute." The hope had turned to hurt. Well, he was a man who had always been counted on to shoot straight from the hip, not pander to feminine sensitivities.

Besides, she thought that wet-behind-the ears young pup was cute?

"I don't give a damn if he was Brad Pitt, you aren't going out with him."

"Clint McPherson, you cannot tell me what to do."

"While you are a guest in my home, I accept responsibility for you. That doesn't include allowing you to go to the movies with a complete stranger."

"Had anybody told you recently you are a real old party pooper?"

"God, I think it's been about seven lovely years since I've heard that."

"Clint," she said, and the tone of her voice changed, "I'll tell you what is not going to happen here. We are not going to have an adult-to-child relationship."

The truth was he was rather hoping they weren't going to have any kind of relationship.

"Great," he said. "I'm all for that. Let's start right now. You can thank me for my hospitality by taking on a few adult responsibilities around here if you plan to stay for a while."

He waited hopefully for her to tilt her nose toward the sky, huff and puff indignantly, and then flounce off to her car and roar out of his life.

She eyed him with a certain shrewdness he didn't care for—as if she detected the beginnings of a plan to get rid of her.

"I have no problem with accepting adult responsibilities," she said, unfortunately choosing to see his words as a challenge rather than an insult. "What would you like me to do? All you have to do is ask. I'm not a mind reader."

Becky chose that moment to start caterwauling, her voice carrying out the nursery window and down across the lawn.

"How would you like to give me a day off?" he said with sudden inspiration. "I'd love to spend a day out on the lake catching some walleye."

"Isn't walleye a kind of disease?" she asked uncertainly.

"It's a kind of fish."

"Ugh, that's just as bad. Worse maybe. Are you going to bring fish here? Slimy? Eyes bugging out? Mouths doing this?"

He watched her mouth contort and her eyes bug out. She was going to make him laugh, damn her.

"Don't forget the full of guts part," he suggested.

"Oh! It must be a guy thing. But sure, go. I'll hold down the fort. What do you want me to do first?"

"I think you'll find, um, *entertaining* Becky will be quite enough of a job."

"See? The trampoline arrived just in time. I can't wait to put her in a dress. She does have dresses, doesn't she? You never seem to get her out of her jammies."

She would know soon enough there was quite a bit more to babies than trampolines and frilly dresses. Whoever invented those wonderful snap-up sleepers should get a Nobel.

The cries from the house were intensifying.

A day on her own with his darling daughter should do for him what he could not do alone. He bet Brandy's bags would be packed before he got home tonight.

"I'd be delighted to give you a day off," Brandy said. "And tell you what. I'll have dinner ready when you get home."

"You do that," he said drily. Leave her with her illusions. The nearest takeout was thirty miles away. And they didn't deliver.

"Oh," she said, "and you don't have to worry about Frankie. I have a boyfriend."

She had a boyfriend? Questions surged into his mind, crowded and slippery, like too many fish in a small pond. Who was it? How old was he? What did he do for a living? What kind of family was he from?

She gave a careless little shrug. "I may marry him. He asked."

He wanted to shake her—or kiss the living daylights out of her! There was a little more to marrying a guy than the fact he had asked. Was there chemistry? Was there respect? Was there love?

For an insane moment, he felt that if he gave into the instinct to kiss her, he would know the answer to each of those questions. And she would know what was supposed to happen between a man and a woman. She would be shaken out of whatever little game she was playing. Brandy King did not look or act like a young woman mooning over a man somewhere.

He leaned toward her.

Her eyes went very wide. Her lips parted. She leaned toward him.

He yanked himself away, furious at himself for his lack of control, but satisfied about what he had just discovered in that momentary lapse of his customary discipline.

Moments later, packing his things into the boat, desperate to be away from her before he asked any of those questions that were swimming furiously in his brain, or worse, took her lips and plundered them, a movement on the front lawn made him turn and look. With Becky in her arms, Brandy was bouncing joyously on the trampoline. His daughter was absolutely shrieking with delight.

Brandy's pajama pants were slipping lower and her camisole higher. Her breasts were doing things that made his mouth go dry. He turned away, knowing he had to get out of there, fast.

It occurred to him he was leaving them without making a single rule about what he considered to be safe behavior on the trampoline.

It occurred to him that deep down he trusted Brandy with his baby, trusted her completely. It didn't make any sense. She was reckless and immature. She might marry a man on the strength of the fact he had *asked*, as if that were all she deserved.

But Clint had always had an unfortunate gift for seeing beyond what she showed the world. He had always caught glimpses of her soul, of a person who was astoundingly deep, blindingly beautiful, breathtakingly sexy.

Oh, his baby was safe enough with Brandy.

It was Clint who was in jeopardy.

Sarah Jane McKenzie stared at the house and shivered, and not because a chill rain was washing over her, turning her dark hair to dripping rope and penetrating her thin, cheap jacket, either.

She was not sure she had ever seen such a house up close. Not that she was that close. She was on the other side of a ten-foot wrought-iron fence that had evil-looking spikes on the top of it.

"To keep the likes of you out," she muttered and shivered again.

The King mansion was like things she'd seen in movies, but never quite believed existed. Majestically situated on the top of a lush rise, it sprawled gloriously. Horses grazed in a grassy paddock in front of it.

She wondered, almost childishly, if there was a swimming pool in the back, and eyed the fence. If she followed its perimeter, could she find out?

"You are not the type of person who prowls fence lines like a common criminal," she told herself proudly.

Then she sighed.

Because the truth was she'd had a terrible sense of not knowing who or what she really was for months now.

Not since Granny Fiona had died. Sarah had unlocked that innocent-looking leather-bound diary, about the nicest thing her granny had owned, and found out that her grandfather was not really Willie McKenzie, ne'er-do-well and town drunk, also dead, though in his case she could not muster any sympathy for the fact.

Willie had been as mean and surly as a too-oft kicked cur, and, if her grandmother's diary was not a lie, her real grandfather was none other than Winston Jacob King.

After a very long debate, Sarah had written him a letter, introducing herself, telling him about finding the diary. It had been kind of a fun letter to write—a letter that had seemed like it was full of potential to make magic things happen to an ordinary girl like her.

She had liked writing it. It had felt as if she were talking to an old friend when she had explained to the stranger who was most likely her real grandfather that he'd had a child with the woman he had loved forty-some-odd years ago.

That child had been her mother, now, sadly, dead, along with every other person in her cursed family.

Writing that letter had made Sarah believe in possibility, something that was pretty foreign in her hard-scrabble world.

In her world, when she'd finished school last June, she'd gone to work full-time as a waitress in the restaurant where she had worked part-time since she was fifteen. It wasn't a fancy place, only a truck stop. There was no money for college, and the fact she had always worked after school meant she did not have the grades to get a scholarship. Not that she would have had the nerve to apply for one anyway. Her family was one tiny step up from trailer trash, and she knew it.

Or had known it until she'd found her grandmother's diary and had realized she really didn't have a single, solitary clue who she was.

A faint and dangerous feeling had fluttered in her breast when she had realized her mother was Jake King's daughter. That feeling had been hope. Hope that maybe the rather dismal landscape of her life could be altered after all. Maybe college wasn't such an unreachable dream. Or a little house with a roof that didn't leak.

Sarah had soon found out it was better never to have hope at all than to have it and then have it quashed.

She had been like a child expecting a letter from Santa Claus, running to the mailbox every day. Her heart had beat faster every single time the phone had rung. But no letter came, and when the phone rang it was the same old thing. The electricity was going to be cut off if she didn't come up with the damn minimum payment.

"Leave it," she had told herself with fierce pride.

But then, in weak moments, like when she saw a picture in the paper of his daughter, Brandy, who looked remarkably like her, she would feel an unfamiliar bitterness well up within her at the total unfairness of life.

She'd tried making excuses for him. Maybe he had never gotten the letter. Maybe it had gotten lost. Maybe you couldn't just write letters to a man like that and expect them to get through.

"Leave it," she'd ordered herself again and again,

ordered herself right until the moment she'd taken all the money she needed to pay the electric bill and had bought a bus ticket instead.

To a place halfway around the East Coast—but really in a totally different world than Hollow Gap, Virginia—on Long Island, New York.

Now she stood outside the fence, way out of view of that gatehouse where the uniformed guard had been reading a book, and realized how foolish it had been to spend her money that way.

There was no way to get near the man. She should take a picture with the cheap throwaway camera she had squandered some of her precious money on and go home. Except she didn't have enough money to get a return ticket.

"Sheesh," she said. "Sarah, you ain't got the brains God give a possum, really."

What was she going to do with a picture of this Southampton mansion? Show it to her friends? Say, "My grandpappy lives here"?

She could almost hear the derisive hoots.

Besides, she wouldn't be showing anything to anybody until she figured out how to get back home. She supposed waitressing jobs weren't any harder to come by here than anywhere else. She'd seen a likely truck stop back there where the bus had stopped.

Still, she'd just follow the fence for a little bit. She'd just follow and see if there was a swimming pool.

Her mama had probably been near forty years old by the time a sister she knew nothing about had been born.

"That's sick," Sarah told herself. "He must have

been near sixty when those other babies were born. He's just a dirty old man. Sarah, you don't want to meet no dirty old man."

But she knew she was just trying to talk herself out of the discouraged feeling that was threatening to well up in her every time she thought of how she had wasted all that money getting here.

She followed the fence through the rain, suddenly aware that she was trying not to cry. Her mama's half sisters had grown up here with horses and guards at the gate and probably a damned swimming pool. She bet it wasn't a little square pool like the public one that opened for a few months every summer in Hollow Gap, either.

And her mama had scrubbed toilets and tried so dad-blamed hard to make ends meet. Was it cancer that had killed her mama? Or hard work, poverty, hopelessness?

The wrought-iron fence followed the curve of a gravel country lane for half a mile or so and then veered inland. Sarah was a long way from the house now, and she realized she might see more horses if she followed the fence, but she doubted if she was going to get a glimpse of the pool.

Though it seemed important to see it. Somehow a private swimming pool symbolized wealth and privilege in a way she could not quite grasp. Somehow the pool would make the lives her aunties had led—and the life she didn't have a hope of obtaining—real to her.

The fence got lost in a tangle of brambles and shrubs, and she pushed through, mainly because she had no other plan, no place to go or be.

On the other side of the brambles, the fence changed

from wrought iron with stone pillars to a huge chain-link affair with barbed wire on top.

"Like you'd see around a prison," she noted, not without satisfaction. Rich people probably lived in a kind of prison, scared of all the poor people. Of course, the ugliness of the fence was shielded from the property by nice hedges and a perimeter of forest.

And then, unexpectedly, Sarah stumbled across a place where the hedge had grown into the fence and weakened it. The fence actually had a hole in it.

Not a big hole, but surely large enough for a little mite of a girl from Virginia to slip through. Without hesitating, because if she hesitated she might lose her nerve, Sarah slipped through the broken fence and walked on her grandfather's land. She was just going to see if there was a swimming pool. That was all. And then she was leaving. No one would ever even know she had been here.

Chapter Three

"Does Becky like bouncing?" Brandy asked, holding the solidness of the baby firmly against her body as she launched all over the surface of the trampoline. She did her best Tigger imitation. "Ba-bounce, ba-bounce, ba-bounce."

What she really wanted to say, to blurt out to Becky and the trees and the whole world was that she was pretty sure Clint McPherson had come within a hair of kissing her.

Brandy wasn't at all sure whether it was the exertion of jumping on the trampoline, a baby the weight of a cannonball in her arms, or that near miss in the kiss department that had her heart hammering so wildly within her chest.

She had come here to Lake of the Woods, to the home of Clint McPherson, she reminded herself sternly—even though it was very difficult to be stern while bouncing on a trampoline with a baby—with a two-part mission.

Part one: to make Clint *feel* something. That goal now seemed exceedingly dangerous.

Part two: to get over the childish crush she once had, which seemed to be totally at odds with part one.

Because how could she get over that crush and be in such close quarters with him every single day? How could she make him feel something and not feel something herself? Just seeing him in his new role as a daddy turned Brandy's insides as warm and soft and mushy as a soufflé fresh out of the oven.

Clint surprised her by being capable of grave tenderness where the baby was concerned. Brandy had caught a look on his face when he'd glanced down at the baby sleeping in his arms, ferocious love mingled with a look at odds with his personality, a look of helplessness.

These glimpses of self-doubt in that self-possessed man made her smile, and made her heart ache for him in the oddest way. Yesterday, she had seen him trying to comb the baby's wild hair—a battle the baby had won rather easily with some lusty yells and sparkling tears.

Just seeing him going through the day, the baby always with him, Clint so big and strong, and the baby so small and delicate, totally melted Brandy's heart. Becky's trust in her "da-da," the way she had him wrapped around her pudgy little finger was both hilarious and endearing. One of her favorite games was to make her father march around the house with her in his arms: she pointed at things autocratically, he obediently named them. Chair. Painting. TV. Stereo. But instead of even attempting to name them, even though it was written all over Clint's face that's what he wanted and hoped for, Becky just pointed her fat little finger at the next item, a small general, very much in charge of her troop of one. No wonder she wasn't walking. She had absolutely no need to!

How could Brandy have a hope of laying to rest a childhood crush when she was seeing Clint in the new and softer light of fatherhood? And now, another complication. How could she lay to rest that childhood crush when she was in imminent danger of being kissed?

She had held out the boyfriend as a defense and it had backfired. She shivered just thinking of the look in Clint's eyes when she had tossed out Jason at him.

What had it been that had flared like fire in the gold of those eyes? Had it been a protective light that had flared to life? So what? A father could be protective. But her woman's intuition told her it had been more than that.

Not exactly jealousy. No, more like possessiveness, though not exactly that either. Suddenly, she had it! In that step toward her, his eyes fastened on her lips, it was as if he had decided she was a child playing at something she knew nothing about, and he was going to show her the real thing.

It should have been insulting, the fact that he so obviously thought she knew nothing about the passions between a man and a woman.

Unfortunately it had more than a bit of truth to it, so instead of being insulted, she had felt eager for the lessons his eyes had promised, had leaned toward him wanting to *know*. The taste of him, the caress of his hand, she had wanted the heat promised in his eyes, to be touched by the flame.

What had made him stop short? His legendary self-control, obviously. But what if she had stepped forward one tiny step? What if she had leaned in just a bit closer? What if she had been bolder?

Dammit, she was supposed to specialize in boldness!

But around Clint, everything she always thought she was seemed to evaporate, her sense of herself seemed to falter.

Brandy bounced higher on the trampoline. Action, movement, energy had always proven balms to a whole wide and wild spectrum of her feelings, from self-doubt to fear.

The baby appreciated the new height and clung to Brandy. "Poo-poo," Becky squealed, using one of her two phrases. "Poo-poo."

"No, no. Trampoline. Tram-po-line."

Brandy decided she didn't care what old Sober-sides thought. The trampoline had been the right move. The baby was ecstatic, gurgling and squealing and laughing. It was the happiest Brandy had ever seen the child, and she was surprised by the strength of her feeling about the baby's reaction: she wanted to make the baby laugh again and again and again.

And, despite the danger involved, she wanted to make Clint laugh! He'd always been a serious man, stern, almost forbidding. But occasionally Brandy had seem him let go, like the time, shortly after he had begun working for her father, that she and her sisters had smuggled a baby goat into the house and it had gone on a rampage. Clint, in camp with her father at the home office, had joined the melee as they had all tried to capture a goat that was not the least bit interested in being captured. It had frolicked through the house, knocking over priceless furniture, breaking lamps, soiling rugs.

Finally, Clint had tackled it, and they had tackled him, everybody trying to get a hand on the slippery goat. The three sisters, the goat and Clint had lain in an untidy pile on the kitchen floor with the cook shaking her spoon at them. They had laughed until Brandy had wondered if you could die from laughing.

Was that the moment she had started to think of Clint in a way that she had never thought of her father's employees? Had realized how handsome he was? Had she longed for that moment, when his warrior eyes glinted with mischief and delight in life, to last forever?

But he had shaken them all off, folded Chelsea's arms around the goat, rumpled Brandy's hair, just to let her know he thought of her as a complete kid, and walked away, still smiling.

Clint and memories of him laughing aside, Brandy was somewhat taken aback by what strong feelings little Becky was eliciting from her after such a short acquaintance. Her scent, the warmth of her solid body, her nature, one minute imperious, the next charming, the sun turning the red curls to bronze—all these things filled Brandy with the loveliest feeling of warmth.

"It's like eating chocolate pudding warm," she decided out loud. The baby's charm and the daddy's rough masculine appeal were combining to make a very dangerous emotional brew here at Clint's lakeside home.

"Poo-poo," the baby squealed again, and Brandy might have taken that for agreement, too, except suddenly the heady sweet scent of the beautiful baby Becky was replaced with quite a different aroma.

The baby hadn't been yelling her excited agreement—she had been making an announcement.

"Please don't leak on me," Brandy said. She quit bouncing and went very still. The baby regarded her solemnly. "Okay, let's find Daddy. His holiday can start right after he looks after this. Clint? Clint? Where are you?"

She looked to the dock, where she had seen Clint out of the corner of her eye the whole time she'd been bouncing. The boat was still tied at the dock, so he hadn't gone yet. Only a moment ago she had seen him crouched down there looking totally enthralled with what appeared to be a bucket of worms. He had also looked exceedingly and disgustingly handsome without half trying, but now he was nowhere to be seen.

Probably watching her discomfort with glee from one of the boathouse windows!

"Clint, not funny!" Her call was louder and more desperate, and another memory of Clint popped out, unbidden from the memory bank. She had been thirteen or fourteen, alone at the pool, when a bug had crawled out of the pool filter. Not any ordinary bug. A monster mutant, shiny and black, the size of her fist.

She had screamed and hopped up on her chair, screamed louder as the bug marched unerringly toward her. Clint had become her hero that day, not because he had come bursting from the house with *that* look on his face—of a warrior who would lay down his own life without hesitation to protect those he cared about—but because he had not laughed at her for being afraid of the bug. By then she was already working tirelessly on the front of being the fearless one, a true tomboy princess, so her gratitude that he had not commented on her panicked state went deep.

In fact, what he had commented on was her swimsuit, not that that suit had ever been intended for swimming. Brandy had felt just a bit of fear when she had put it on, too, because it was an experiment with being a girl. But it had made her look way too grown-up, and she wasn't at all sure what she would do if a boy—or a man—had treated her like a grown-up.

But Clint had squished the bug, heard her confession of fear and looked at the bathing suit without his expression altering over any of those three things.

"Go change into something else," he'd said in a voice that brooked no discussion.

What a relief that had been—even if she had given him a dirty look and marched away with her nose in the air.

Not that this was the same thing, even though she could certainly hear a little of the same shrillness in her voice as she called to him to come get his now very stinky daughter.

"How can somebody so very small make such a very large smell?" Brandy muttered.

Becky smiled angelically at her.

"Where's your father?"

"Da-da," she said and stuck her thumb in her mouth.

"You shouldn't put anything—not even your own

thumb—in your mouth with a smell like that in the air. It's got to be laden with germs." Brandy held her own breath just in case. After a while, it occurred to her there was no hero dashing to her rescue and that if she did not breathe soon she might faint and fall on top of the baby. And who knew what might squish out of her?

She held the baby at arm's length and called again.

The baby's legs began to churn the air, which was definitely not a good thing. The pudgy whirring legs acted just like a fan for that atrocious smell. And, if Brandy was not mistaken, all that activity was putting all the wrong things in motion. The padding around those tubby little legs was beginning to swell with a mysterious brown substance, held in only by very flimsy-looking elastic banding.

"I'm going to be sick," Brandy warned her.

"Poo-poo," Becky told her pleasantly.

"Thank you. I've figured that much out. Cllliinnnnt!"

Silence.

Carefully, after reviewing her limited options, Brandy realized she was going to have to do something.

"One step at a time," she told herself, trying to sound brave. "Get off the trampoline."

She set the baby on the surface of the trampoline and hopped down onto the ground.

"Don't get any of that on my new trampoline," she warned Becky.

Becky apparently had her own idea of how the trampoline should be christened. Taking a deep breath Brandy picked up the baby and, holding her straight-armed in front of herself, dashed madly for the house.

"Step two, find the change room."

She had never been upstairs, but she guessed, from the window the shrieking had emerged from this morning, which door held a nursery.

Despite her anxious state, she noticed Clint's upstairs decor was much the same as that downstairs—the perfection, personality and cleanliness of a very expensive hotel room.

"Step two," she reminded herself, bursting through a door. The nursery was lovely. Everything was pristine white and lacy. The walls, the crib, the carpets, the gauzy curtains that hung at the windows were all white.

The effect was dreamy and vaguely cold. Had Rebecca designed this room? Was it wrong to feel dislike for a woman who was dead?

"A little color is a good thing," Brandy muttered.

"Poo-poo," the baby agreed.

"Well, maybe not that color."

The change area had been as well thought out as the rest of the nursery. It was in an adjoining room, as white and sterile as a hospital surgery.

"Step three." Oh, God. Remove the diaper? Was there any other way? Brandy laid the baby on the change table and began to take inventory.

"Quit wagging your legs," she ordered sternly.

The baby paid her no heed.

The room was obviously well stocked. There were stacks of disposable diapers, clean sleepers, creams and ointments and powders and wet wipes and cotton swabs. But she did not see any of the essentials, items she absolutely had to have—rubber throwaway gloves, face masks, scented room spray.

She got her hands on a bottle of baby powder and squeezed. A plume of white powder temporarily masked the odor coming from the baby.

She tried one last time. "Clint!"

She heard the throaty growl of a boat starting. It was akin to the cavalry leaving instead of arriving. With one hand firmly on the baby, she leaned over and pried the window open. It faced the lake, and she saw Clint back the boat away from the pier and then power up. Its nose heaved out of the water and it left a foaming wake behind it.

The man at the helm looked happy and relaxed, and not the least interested in the damsel in distress he had just abandoned.

Brandy stared after the departing boat, then glanced at the baby. She made the mistake of taking a deep breath.

"I'm going to cry," she decided. "Right after I throw up." She squeezed the baby-powder bottle again.

The baby beat her to the crying stage. Her enjoyment of her stinky situation evaporated with unfair swiftness. Her tiny features screwed up and she began to scream her indignation at being left in this state.

Brandy started to take another deep breath, but caught herself. Hand still on the squirming baby, she stuck her head out the window, gulped some air, then held her breath. She turned back to Becky, squeezed the powder bottle for good measure, and tried to decide on a good way to approach step three—diaper removal.

After pondering it for a few seconds, she realized a good way probably did not exist. She steeled herself, pried the first tab open, squeezed the baby-powder bottle. The room was beginning to be filmed with a fine white substance, but that was the least of her problems.

"I need to see this as an opportunity," she shouted to herself over the howls of the baby. "This is a time to correct misinterpretations. Clint has made it clear that he thinks I am spoiled and useless and out of touch with reality."

Of course, if this was reality, who needed it? Though no doubt he would think a *real* woman would know how to change a diaper.

He hadn't voiced any judgments of her, but she could see them in his eyes, in the downward quirk of that handsome mouth, in the muscle that leaped in his jaw when he was impatient or displeased.

Maybe, instead of viewing this as her worst nightmare come to life, she could turn it around. Prove her competence at dealing with what, for many women, would be the most ordinary of life situations.

Oh, yes, wouldn't it change his opinion of her if she presented him with a baby who was sparkling clean? Not just in clean diapers! Oh, no. She'd even dress the baby up. And maybe herself. And comb the baby's hair, and her own. She'd promised him dinner. She hadn't missed the look of cynical doubt on his face, as if he didn't think she could pull that off. Wouldn't that amaze and astound him if she could?

Okay, it would amaze and astound her, too!

But, wait! What was she thinking?

"You don't want to change his opinion of you,"

Brandy reminded herself firmly. "What you want to do is change your opinion of him."

But she'd been here four days and nothing was changing.

In fact, watching his awkward and tender efforts to cope with all the ins and outs of single-parenting seemed to be making what she had always felt for him feel more intense.

"I do not love Clint McPherson," she told herself grimly.

Still, what, other than love, could make a person change a diaper that was now leaking foul brown material all over the lovely quilted white top of the change table?

"Maybe I love you," Brandy told the baby, hoping this proclamation might stem the unholy shrieks coming from the baby's tiny little mew of a mouth.

This was the problem. Obviously she did not love the baby, not yet. But how long would it take, foul odors aside? If she stayed much longer, it was apparent attachments were going to form. She had known it was a bad idea to come here, had known it with her whole heart and soul.

"Poo-poo," Becky screamed, as if she thought added volume might get the message across to the dull-witted girl who was not doing any of the things that normally were done for a soiled baby.

"Never mind poo-poo. I know that much already."

She found the second tab on the diaper, took a deep breath, like a soldier who had just been ordered over the top, and unhinged it. The diaper sprang open with unholy enthusiasm, aided by Becky's wildly flapping limbs. Brandy closed her eyes to remove it, which may have been a mistake, because the baby's foot ended up in the worst of it and splashed up a vicious spray that splattered the walls and the front of Brandy's pajamas.

Why hadn't her father asked her sister Jessica to come here to Clint's rescue? Jessie would be so much more suited to this present activity. Jessie had actually dissected the baby pig in biology class and had lived to talk about it.

She was rational, calm, smart. Pragmatic. Clint had always liked her and respected her.

Half an hour later, with poo-poo just about everywhere but on the light fixtures, covered in baby-powder dust, Brandy had her cell phone in her hand.

She sat on the floor of the change room, in a litter of wrecked diapers, while the baby, happy again, but bare butt to the air, crawled around on the floor.

"Jessica King, please. I don't care if she's teaching a class. This is her sister Brandy and this is an emergency."

It seemed like a long time before she heard her sister's voice on the line.

"Brandy? What's wrong? What's happened?"

She felt a moment's guilt that she'd worried her sister.

She explained the diaper dilemma. "And once the baby is wet, and you have the petroleum jelly on your hands, the new diaper tabs won't stick. Or maybe it's the baby powder. I tried tying the darn thing on with the drapery string, but that didn't work either." She sent a somewhat contrite look at the venetian blinds that were now puddled on the window sill.

There was a long silence on the other end of the phone.

"Let me get this straight. The last I heard you were bungee-basing in Hungary—"

"BASE jumping in Venezuela," Brandy corrected her.

"And so I naturally assumed that an emergency meant you had finally managed to break your cotton-pickin' neck, but really you're with Clint McPherson, at his remote house, on Lake of the Woods? In Canada?"

"That's right."

"With Clint?" she asked again.

"Well, I mean not with him—"

"You know, as much as I would love to hear all the details of how you ended up playing house with the man you've had a crush on since you were three—"

"That's not true. I didn't know him when I was three." Hastily she addressed the larger issue. "I do not have a crush on him. I hate him!"

"Same thing. I can't believe you had me called from class for this. Where's Clint?"

"I offered to give him a day off to catch diseased fish."

"You're not even making sense. Are you on something?"

Her sister knew better than that. "I may have inhaled baby powder," she said proudly, and then more desperately, "Jess, I always call on you when my rational mind fails me. Because you got the rational for all three of us."

"If you ever called me when your rational mind failed you, there would not be any bunbasing off buildings."

If her sister was so smart how come she couldn't remember what BASE stood for, even though Brandy had told her a million times. BASE: building, antenna, span and earth. Now might not be the time to ask, because Brandy thought she detected a certain softening in her sister's tone.

"So, do you know how to get the diaper to stay on, to stick?" she asked.

"No, but if I do an experiment that fails, I have to back it up step by step until I find the mistake where things started to go off track."

That would be when I agreed to come here.

"That would be when I misinterpreted the cries of poo-poo for joy at the new trampoline I bought. For the baby."

"You bought a baby a trampoline? Are you crazy?" Her sister sighed. "Never mind. What an idiotic question to ask someone who has seen Angel Falls from such a thrilling perspective."

It occurred to Brandy that her sister Jessica, intelligent, calm, sane, rational, would probably be a much better match for Clint than she herself was. But Jessie had some kind of relationship with a bookish guy, Professor Mitch Michaels, at the university.

Chelsea and Brandy both hated him, though they were careful not to let their sister know her beau seemed dull, intellectually snobby, and had an air of annoying superiority about him. Jess deserved so much better.

Not that Brandy kidded herself that she was any kind of expert on relationships, and not that she was matching herself with Clint. And not that her sister, even if she was available, would ever consider Clint, knowing the unspoken truth about how Brandy felt about him. She felt a warm appreciation for her sisters.

"How's Chelsea?" she asked.

"Brandy, we can't make this a social call! I'm in the middle of teaching a class. I'm a member of the real world."

Good. Her sister didn't want to visit. That meant she wouldn't have to inquire about Mitch. Still, she had to ask. "And Chelsea and I aren't? Members of the real world?"

Her sister snorted and focused on the task at hand rather than answering. "The diaper? How can I help you with something like that? I'm a million miles away. Are you close to the Internet?"

"It helps just hearing your voice," Brandy admitted. "I feel calmer already. Here's what happened…so now the baby is damp, and I have something on my hands that is waterproof and that makes the diaper tabs useless."

"Duct tape," her sister decided.

"What?"

"Thick gray tape, in a roll."

"He'll have that?"

"He's a man. He'll have it."

Her sister had always seemed rather bookish, and her so-called boyfriend worse. How did she know what regular guys had and didn't have? She'd probably read it in a book.

"Poo-poo," the baby crowed, making a grab for the phone.

"That was the baby with her personal rendition of hello," Brandy explained.

"She sounds adorable."

Brandy heard a softening in her sister's voice, a

yearning, that took her by surprise, even though she was dealing with that very yearning herself.

"Don't be fooled. She is a poo-poo manufacturing menace."

"Okay, Brandy, find some duct tape. If that doesn't work, maybe an elastic band or something. A big one. If worse comes to worse put her in some of those rubber baby pant things and stuff them with paper towels."

"Hey, that's good," Brandy said admiringly. She reached for a pair of rubber pants. "Don't hang up! I'll try with you on the line." Brandy clamped the cell phone between her ear and her shoulder.

"How is Clint?" Jessie asked, as Brandy, tongue caught between her teeth, began to stuff the baby into the rubber pants and then paper padding into the pants.

"He's fine," she said tersely.

"He looked terrible at the funeral."

She didn't want to hear about his overwhelming grief for the woman he had married instead of her.

"Not that I ever, even once, entertained the notion of marrying him."

"What?"

"Nothing!"

"Oh, Brandy!"

There was just a little too much sympathetic knowing in that last comment.

"Well, this seems like it will do just fine. You're a ge-nius! Thanks for your help, Jessica. Bye."

She set down the cell and heard a door slam, feet coming up the steps.

"Brandy? Becky?"

"Be quiet," she told the baby. She did not want to be seen like this.

The baby was terrible at following instructions. "Da-da," she screamed. "Da-da!"

"Brandy?"

Brandy said a word that meant poo-poo. The door swung open.

"I forgot my fishing license. I just came back—" his voice died in this throat.

Suddenly she saw what this little room must look like through his eyes. Discarded diapers, turned inside out and backward until they looked like mutated marshmallows, were scattered over every available space. There were unsightly brown blotches on many surfaces, including Brandy's chest. Baby powder covered everything, like a fine dusting of fresh snow. The blinds were ripped down. Brandy's own appearance, she knew, would be disheveled. She felt sweaty and sticky and out of sorts.

It was really not one of her finer moments.

Clint folded his arms across his chest, rocked back on his heels and regarded her steadily.

"I'm just about done," she said regally.

"I can see that. And when you're done here there's another room I've been thinking of having demolished."

There was a suspicious glint in his eye.

"Don't laugh," she warned him, forgetting entirely that had been part of the *mission*.

"I'm not."

"I see tears in the corners of your eyes."

"Fumes."

"I did my best."

"I don't doubt it for a minute."

"There!" Triumphantly, she slipped the last of the paper padding into the rubber pants. She lifted the baby for his inspection.

"What exactly is that?" Clint asked carefully.

"It's ingenuity at its finest," Brandy told him dangerously.

"It looks like she's wearing a pumpkin. A lumpy, white pumpkin."

He came and took the baby from her. Was there something just a little bit protective in how he did it?

His shoulders were shaking, and his lips twitched upward.

And then, despite his obvious effort at restraint, he was laughing! It sounded wonderful, deep and rich and carefree. He threw back his head and laughed, and she could have enjoyed it so much more if he weren't laughing at her!

She remembered the object had been to get him to laugh, but this wasn't at all what she'd had in mind, though maybe it was totally worth it.

"It's my fault," he choked out finally, wiping the tears from his eyes with the back of his hand. "I forgot how terrible those first few solo diaper changes are. I used duct tape once."

"That gray stuff," Brandy said knowledgeably, wondering when the heck her sister had become such an expert on men. She couldn't believe it would have anything to do with Mitch.

"That's the stuff. Several times me and the baby had

to hit the shower after the whole procedure. Covered from head to toe, just the whites of our eyes showing."

Brandy laughed. Only minutes ago she had wondered if she would ever laugh again. Hadn't this always been Clint's gift? He made things that were wrong, right. He didn't even try to do it. He just did. He had an instinct for the right word, the right gesture.

He reached out now and chucked Brandy on the chin, as if they were members of the same team who had just survived a life-threatening mission.

"You're a good sport," he told her.

It was hardly *I'll love you endlessly,* but even the faintest of praise, the faintest hint of approval from him, did heady and dangerous things to her.

"Oh, go catch your fish," she said, reaching for the baby.

"You know," he said doubtfully, keeping the baby, "I could stay. I don't think the walleye are biting today, anyway."

"Don't you dare feel sorry for me," she said. What would be worse than his pity?

"I don't, but—"

But. That famous word that canceled out whatever had preceded it.

"This is not too much for me," she said. "This is just a glitch. The day can't do anything but get better, right?"

"Right." The doubt remained in his voice.

"Go. I can handle this. I find it very insulting that you think I'm useless."

"I never said that."

"I can see it in your eyes."

"Don't even think you can guess what you see in my eyes," he said quietly. He took a step toward her.

She held her breath because, for a danger-filled moment, her every instinct had shouted, *He's going to kiss me.*

It was the second time within as many hours.

But, for the second time, he didn't. The light she had seen faded from his eyes so quickly she knew she must have been mistaken in thinking she had seen it.

Instead, he relinquished the baby to her. "I'll stay," he decided. "Just for a bit. I'll show you how to put on a diaper and a few other essentials for living with a baby."

"Such as?" she asked haughtily.

"Do you know what a washing machine is?"

"Vaguely."

"Microwave?"

"Yes!"

He kicked up a puff of baby powder. "Vacuum cleaner?"

"Uh—"

"Okay, well, we'll start with a load of laundry because it kind of looks like you're going to need to do one."

Both their eyes went to the big brown stain on the front of her nice yellow pajama top.

"I'm sure I can manage."

"Have you ever done laundry?" he pressed.

"Zillions of times," she lied. She'd grown up a King, doing laundry meant placing soiled items in the laundry hamper. They were returned clean. Not much had changed when she traveled. Laundry was placed in the laundry bag in her room.

"You're a terrible liar," he told her softly.

Then now would be the wrong time to tell him, again, that she wanted him to go. Because she didn't. She didn't want him to go at all.

Chapter Four

"This is fun."

Clint slid Brandy a look to see if she was kidding, but Brandy was apparently genuinely enjoying herself.

Looking at her, he realized he had gotten himself into a troublesome situation. Because there was an astoundingly attractive woman standing beside him in the rather close confines of his laundry room. She was at ease in one of his white button-down shirts and nothing else. The shirt swam around her, the tails ending at the tanned curves of her thighs. She'd worn shorts shorter than that shirt, but the result had not been as devastatingly sexy.

Strangely, swathed in a man's shirt, the tomboy image was erased. She looked exquisitely feminine, and just a little too much as if they had shared an experience quite a bit more exciting and intimate than cleaning up after a baby's diaper change gone terribly wrong. She still had a dusting of baby powder clinging to the shiny mass of her untamed hair.

Right now Brandy had the tip of her lovely pink tongue caught between her small white teeth and was measuring laundry detergent carefully into the washer.

"I thought you'd done this zillions of times," he reminded her, juggling the baby to his other hip. "You'd think it would be just a little less fun by a zillion and one."

"Oh, sure," she said. She stuck that delectable tongue out at him. "And it was fun all those times, too. You sound like Dr. Seuss." Her voice changed to a happy little singsong. "It's a little less fun at a zillion and one."

She was trying to divert him from the fact he had caught her in a lie. Brandgwen King had very obviously never done a load of laundry in her entire privileged existence.

"If I sound like Dr. Seuss, it's from reading to the baby," he said, not diverted. What was going on here? One of the wealthiest young women in the world was enjoying doing laundry? Sincerely thought it was fun?

She ducked his piercing gaze, and her voice was still light and cheerful, the voice of someone very practiced at the art of diversion. "Oh! You read to Becky. I can just picture the two of you all cuddled up in that big chair in front of the fireplace, her cooing and grabbing for the book. How adorable!"

Though the picture was amazingly accurate, and he looked forward to those rare quiet moments with his daughter when the mountains of work were done, he took exception to Brandy's phrasing. *Adorable?* If he had a least favorite word in the English language that had to be it—particularly in reference to any activity of his.

Unfortunately this was his burden to bear—women thought single dads were adorable. Still, he tried to defend himself. "Reading promotes language development."

"I suppose you're reading her *War and Peace* or something equally as *developmental*, Sober-sides."

"Dr. Seuss," he responded, in denial of the Sober-sides title, a guy who knew how to have some fun with his reading material. He realized he'd walked into a trap when she crowed triumphantly.

"I told you! Adorable. The two of you cuddled up with *Green Eggs and Ham*." She sighed happily at the picture of domestic bliss she was creating.

He shot her another look. Under that globe-hopping adventure seeker, did Brandy crave a different lifestyle? He smelled danger.

Still, the part of him that was pure male was offended. Given what she was wearing, *adorable* sounded like an insult, as if he were a big, wonderful teddy bear, safe and without teeth.

Wasn't that exactly what he was striving to be around her? He reminded himself sternly that she was not just immature, she was totally off-limits.

He decided to try and shift the focus back from his and the baby's adorable reading program to her lies—and not the one about laundry, either. The bigger one—the one she was telling with her life.

"One would wonder," he said, choosing his words with care, "why you have to race cars and horses, climb ice, white-water canoe, helicopter ski and throw yourself into thin air when you have fun doing such simple things."

"Oh," she turned and grinned at him. "I had no idea you were keeping track of my activities. I'm flattered."

The grin was another diversionary tactic.

"Don't be," he said. "Your father talks about his girls endlessly."

"Oh."

Did she look, and sound, disappointed that his interest in her was not personal? That he was not tracking her adventures and misadventures in the tabloids? And was it completely true that he wasn't?

Didn't he buy every piece of newsprint that had her picture or name on it? Didn't he turn up the sound on the television if they flashed her picture across the screen? Damn. She was good at this diversionary stuff. Because he was beginning to wonder about his own motive in delving into her life.

Brandy began dropping items for laundry load number two, carefully sorted by color, into the foaming water.

"You still haven't answered the question," he reminded her, not fooled by her expression of total engrossment in her task. "If you can have fun doing simple things like bouncing on a trampoline with a baby, doing a load of laundry, why are you out cruising the world for all the thrills it can offer?"

"That's not about fun, really," she offered, but reluctantly.

"No? What's it about then, Brandy?"

She glanced at him, uncomfortable, then looked swiftly back to her laundry. "Who knows?" she said, a tiny snap in her voice.

His own inner voice warned him to leave it. The last thing he needed to do was probe the complexities of the very complex Miss King. It was a job that could take a lifetime and only be just begun.

Still, he could not leave it. It wasn't just him she was outrunning. It was herself. Could he make the real Brandy King stand up?

"Who knows?" he pressed. "You know."

She glared at him, shrugged, frowned furiously at the clothes she was dropping in the water. "Adrenaline," she finally admitted. "That's not the same as fun. It's intense. Live-or-die kind of stuff. It makes life feel important. It makes me feel alive."

He heard the unspoken. It made her feel important. Which begged the question, how did she feel most of the time? Didn't her so-called boyfriend make her feel important and alive?

The answer had revealed more than he wanted to know. She was young and attractive; she was well traveled; she could have anything in the whole world, just by pointing her finger at it.

And nothing had filled her. She was empty and disconnected, searching not for adventure, but for herself.

Not that he wanted to know even that much. He had already probed enough. Knowing more about her would just add to that sense he always had that there was Brandy, as she showed herself to the world, and then there was Brandy as he saw her, and he was pretty sure which one was true and real.

It just might be this girl beside him who was delighting in watching as the washer filled with hot soapy water.

"Bleach?" she asked enthusiastically, eager to change the subject. "In this little spout, right?"

He rescued the bleach from her before she managed to pour it.

"For the whites and badly stained stuff. Now that the stinkies have been dispensed with we can probably live without the bleach."

"Clint, who would have ever thought fate held this for you! You've become an expert on bleach!"

There was no judgment in her voice, only genuine amazement.

It was true, though, no one really knew what life held for them, even a person like him, who had had everything so carefully planned, who had lived and breathed the illusion he was in control.

"So, is this your life? The baby? Laundry? Cooking, cleaning…"

"Don't forget fishing and flowers," he said drily. "PTA, church choir, arachnid enthusiasts of the Internet…"

She ignored his attempt at humor. "Aren't you bored?" she demanded.

He could point out that he still worked for her father, but his reduced schedule was hardly challenging.

Just as he did not want to probe the inner secrets of her world, he did not want the inner secrets of his probed.

Was he bored? Or contented? Or just going through each day as an automaton, doing his best to survive a difficult situation, doing what was required of him? He was a warrior without a war, though he suspected, that just like Brandy, his greatest battlefield was not out there, in the world, at all.

It was within himself.

Rebecca had died in a terrible car crash just days after they'd had the baby christened. It had thrown him into a world he was ill prepared to deal with, a world where another person totally depended on him. It had fractured his confidence, his belief he could control his world, that he was strong, infallible, in charge.

Rebecca's death and the baby's dependence had humbled him.

On the other hand, he could thank God he'd had something to learn and someone to be responsible for. Otherwise he might have perished himself. And not of a broken heart, either, though he knew that's what everyone wanted to believe.

No. Guilt. Guilt that his heart was not broken.

Guilt that he had made such a bad mistake in marrying Rebecca.

"Okay," he said, deftly sidestepping Brandy's question and returning his attention to the washing machine. "That's that."

He reached by her and shut the lid on the washer. "When it's finished, you—"

"I know. I'm a quick study. I take it out and put it in the dryer. But only after reading the label."

"Okay, we've mastered the microwave and the washer and dryer, the wind-up rocking chair-swing for Becky, formula and diapers and the scientific mixing of pablum. We've vacuumed the baby powder. Is that enough for one day?"

She was looking at him in a way that was very disconcerting.

The same way he had looked at her only an hour or so ago in the baby change room.

As if she could find out who he really was if she wanted to. As if she planned to take his lips between hers and devour him.

It had been that way between them since just before she'd turned nineteen, the sudden uncontrollable leaping of electricity in the air, unmistakable chemistry.

But the truth was the same now as it had been then. Brandy King was taboo.

She was far too young for him, thirteen years his junior. But more, her father had placed his trust in him. Jake King trusted him to be good and decent, and, above all things, an honorable man. That anyone would have that expectation of Clint, given his rough-and-tumble background, had made him want to be more than he had ever been before.

The hired hands did not seduce the daughters of their bosses. It was a "thou shalt not" in Clint's eyes. The fact that the thought even crossed his mind, around Brandy, then and now, filled him with a kind of self-disgust.

He had come from chaos. His number-one love in life was control. Why did this little slip of a girl with her wayward hair and her mischievous sapphire-shaded eyes threaten that control so completely?

On the other hand, all that control, his very best thinking, had not exactly achieved the result he would have expected, or at least not in his personal life.

He had selected a wife as analytically as he would have searched out a good business prospect. He knew the statistics on marriage. Nearly fifty percent of them ended in failure. *Failure* was not part of his vocabulary.

Rebecca and he had dated on and off for a year or so. She had been smart, calm, cool, collected, classy and beautiful to boot.

She was the one who had suggested marriage. There had been talk of a biological clock, but not of love. There had been agreement on common interests and goals, but there had been no chasing each other around the kitchen table until they were both breathless with laughter.

There had not been great chemistry, but he had regarded that volatile ingredient with suspicion. Anything seemed better than allowing passion to rule over reason. He'd lived with the results of that his entire life: his mother and father's early passion long since metamorphosed into an ugly and ceaseless rage at each other. But, looking back on his own choices, had all Clint's careful and passionless planning brought a better result? No. His marriage had been hell, only without the heat.

He had not realized how he longed for closeness, for true intimacy, until he had realized his marriage was a cold place to go home to. Rebecca seemed to *like* distance, to resent his efforts to close the emotional chasms between them. Not that he wanted to blame Rebecca. He had brought a whole shipload full of inadequacies to that union.

No, after the excruciating loneliness of his last union, Clint had vowed, he was not doing the marriage thing again. If statistics meant anything, and he trusted that they did, his lack of parental modeling and his lack of success, however private, in his first venture marked him for future failure.

He was concentrating now, fully and completely, on raising a daughter who would have a better chance at emotional success than he had. But if she had never seen a good relationship, would his daughter be able to find one?

He had grown to hate how every choice he made, now that he was a father, reverberated with possible future repercussions for his daughter.

"Clint?"

He shook his head, came back to the moment. Brandy's slender hand was on his arm. She had one bare leg tucked behind the other. Her toes were cute, painted a surprising shade of gum ball–pink.

The problem with Brandy—it had always been the problem with Brandy—was that his mind just went places he simply did not allow it to go, like a wild horse that had been tamed, but not quite as completely as anyone thought.

"Sorry," he said. "I was thinking." *I have to get out of here.* "I'm going to go fishing now, if that's all right with you. If you feel ready to take over."

"Okay, I'm ready." She held out her arms to the baby. "Go fishing. And don't worry about a thing. I'm looking forward to being in charge. I even still plan to get dinner ready."

Actually, given the state of the change room after her attempt at diapers, he wondered what she could do to his kitchen. Brandy cooking sounded like a cause for real concern, not that, given the happy light that shone in her face, he could tell her that.

"Uh, there's frozen entrées in the freezer. Your dad has the cook send them to me in monthly batches."

"Thank God you aren't adding gourmet cooking to your list of enthusiasms! I was beginning to think you were a superhero."

"Well, we both know nothing could be further from the truth than that." He felt, fully, the weight of his failures.

"Do we?" she asked softly, sincerely, and there was just the faintest hint of seduction on her breath. She leaned toward him.

"If we don't, we should," he said, turning abruptly away from her.

"Oh, please don't—"

He waited for her to finish the sentence with the word *go*. If she asked him to stay, would he, even though he knew he was like that moth, flirting ever closer to the flame?

"—catch any fish," she said.

Relief swept him. He tried to tell himself there was no regret mingled with that relief. He tried to hide his confusion with a teasing tone. "Your real-world experience really won't be complete until you clean a fish."

"Ugh."

She was so cute when she said *ugh!* Her nose screwed up and her eyes nearly crossed.

He struggled to keep it light. "After dirty diapers, believe me, scaling and gutting a fish is a piece of cake."

"Stop it," she pleaded. "You'll make me gag again. I think I've had enough of that for one day."

He realized, despite his deepest desire to back away from her and erect a wall between them, he fell into teasing her as naturally as he breathed. And the banter didn't ease the sensual tension that leaped up between them. It supplemented it.

Again, it was such a contrast to his married life. He and Rebecca hadn't been able to talk together in any way that had seemed *real*. Communication had always seemed stilted. They hadn't argued, ever, but had lived together in a prison of loneliness that had been somehow just as devastating as his mother and father's bickering had been. He had harbored the hope that the baby would help build a bridge between them.

Now, seeing the reality of the baby, the daily grind, the exhaustion, he knew Becky would not have healed whatever had gone wrong between him and her mother.

"Have fun," Brandy called after him.

But Clint went back out to his boat, uneasy.

A little more than a year since his wife's death, and he had not yet explored his feelings. Of course, exploring feelings was not in his nature. He'd grown up in a world where feelings were for sissies, a sign of weakness.

Yet, suddenly it felt as though Brandy's presence in his life was going to force him to look at his unfinished business.

He felt nothing but resentment. It should have felt wonderful to have an afternoon to himself, away from the ceaseless demands of his tiny tyrant of a daughter and from the subtle temptation of Brandy's constant presence in his well-ordered life.

But even as he piloted the boat into the open water and began the very scientific business of setting his hooks, his mind kept drifting to Brandy. What was she doing now? Had she changed out of that shirt yet? He should have left more instructions. Don't touch the iron under any circumstances. The microwave will not dry clothes.

Instead he had run scared, from the look in her eyes. But he hadn't really left the look behind. It dogged him, and he had to fight the compulsion to turn around and go back to her, to the promise of laughter and companionship. The aloofness he wore around himself was a shield, and she could break it down. If he let her. So, naturally, he deliberately stayed on the water much longer than he normally would have.

He tried not to see the lake through her eyes, tried not to wonder how she would have reacted to its immenseness, to all its secret coves and dark brooding beauty.

He wondered if she would have liked to put ashore there and roast wieners. Rebecca had not been a roasting-wieners kind of girl, but he suspected Brandy would be. When the first fish bit, he imagined her horror and squeals. He wondered what it would be like to help her catch her first fish. Would he put her arms around her to help her reel it in?

Stop it, he ordered himself sternly. He was going to treat her like his kid sister, period. He was going to use the entire force of his will toward that goal.

The problem was that many years ago, Brandy King had kissed him, and it had changed everything.

It had been like touching a flame. It had threatened his well-honed sense of control like nothing else in his life. It had felt downright dangerous.

She had been nineteen. That had been way too much power for a nineteen-year-old to wield over a mature man.

He had done what he'd had to do. He had rejected her with intentional cruelty.

And when Rebecca had invited him to share her world, he had thought it a safety zone. She was a woman as cool and collected and as in control as he himself was. What a shock that all his careful planning, his control, had not brought the predicted result at all.

His marriage simply had not been a happy one.

A long time ago, he had touched a flame, and had backed away from it before it had burned him alive. Still, hadn't he longed for it? Yearned for that feeling of being so alive? So on the edge? Wasn't that exactly how Brandy had just said she felt when she jumped from high places?

Danger. He had recognized that from the start. But hadn't that one kiss become so much a part of what he was that he had named this quiet lakeside retreat Touch the Flame when it was so obviously a choice in exactly the other direction?

Fishing, he decided, was simply the wrong activity for a man with a lot on his mind. It allowed too much time for thinking. Too much time for trying to figure out the ins and outs of life.

He headed back to his dock. The last of the light was leeching from the day as he docked the boat. He turned and looked at his house.

It was almost completely lit up. It looked like such a warm place, the flowers bright in the fading light, the house's golden lights sending ribbons of welcome out against the dark water. It created an illusion, like a picture on a greeting card, of the kind of place every man

in the world yearned to come home to. That new trampoline on the lawn made it easy to imagine children playing, the evening air ringing with shouts and laughter.

He scoffed at himself for allowing himself to believe
such nonsense. His own childhood had rung with shouts,
all right. Combat. Chaos.

That girl, reckless, irresponsible, irrepressible, charming, had managed to touch him in that deep place within
himself that he'd thought did not exist anymore.

A place where hope lived in secret.

A place that he wanted to believe in for his daughter,
if not for himself.

Still, he steeled himself against the lure of that hope,
the yearning that felt like a weakness in his soul.

He had started the day planning to get rid of her. He
would end it the same way.

"Sarah, my dear, would you tell James I'd like tea?"

Sarah looked up from the desk she was working at.
The desk was old and antique, probably worth a million
dollars, and he had brought it into his office just for her.

Tea she knew was a euphemism for medication.
Though Jake King had not said so in so many words,
she knew he was ill. Very ill.

Sometimes she still could not believe how she came
to be sitting here, sharing this office with her grandfather, or how easy it had been to get here.

Not that he knew that he was her grandfather.

That day when she had decided just to have a look
at the pool had proved fateful. Because there had been
a pool, and she had decided irrationally that she was

going to swim in her grandfather's pool if it was the last thing she ever did. That day had been too wet and a gardener had been working within sight. Sarah had needed a plan if she was going to swim there.

She left the estate and went back to town, found a cheap motel room, paid some of her precious dollars, waited and plotted, determined her chance would come.

And then early, early the next morning, before anyone would be up in that grand house, she was sure, she crept back there, back through the hole in the fence and across those emerald-green lawns. The sun was out, but it was cold. She prayed the water was heated.

She hadn't brought a bathing suit with her to Southampton, so her plan was to strip down to her under things, swim, then go back to where she belonged and never give this place or her link to it another thought or a backward glance.

But to her consternation there was an old man sitting beside the pool, wrapped in blankets, waiting for the dawn. He spotted her before she could creep away.

"You there," he commanded imperiously, "what are you doing? What do you want?"

She felt like a deer, caught in headlights. She wanted to bolt, but she was frozen. She forced herself to smile, to move jauntily toward him.

She knew it was Jacob King. She had sought out and found his picture many times since reading her grandmother's diary.

"I was looking for the service entrance. I wanted to apply for a job."

"Come here," he beckoned with knobbly old fingers,

and she thought again of bolting, but she didn't. It was as if an invisible thread, iron-strong, pulled her closer to him.

She went to him and looked into eyes startlingly like her own—dark brown fringed with black.

He studied her, and she sensed his shrewdness, but she also sensed the thing she was least expecting of Jacob King. Kindness.

He patted the deck chair next to him, and she braced herself to be asked how she had gotten in here, but he didn't ask that. He asked how old she was and where she was from and what kind of work she had done in the past. Before she knew, it she had told him quite a lot about herself—almost everything except the real reason she was here.

"I think I may have a job for you," he said thoughtfully, but then paused and watched, with a kind of reverence, as the sun came up.

He sighed and turned back to her. "I want somebody to sort photographs of my family for me, put them in order, choose the best of them and make albums for my daughters. Could you do that?"

Fear filled her. It was on the tip of her tongue to say no. She had never done anything like that. She had worked in restaurants all her life and not even good ones. She probably wasn't suited to a sit-down kind of a job. She was here under false pretenses, and he was bound to find that out.

Still, she was here. She wanted something, and she did not even know what it was. She knew down to her gut that if she turned away from this opportunity, she might never know, and that it would sit in her like a monster and feed on her insides.

"I guess I could try it," she said, and then, not wanting to appear like a pushover, or as desperate as she was, she added with false confidence, "if the money was right."

He patted her hand, just as if he saw right through that false confidence, and said, "And what would that be, my dear?"

She named a figure she considered absurd—twelve dollars an hour. She wished she'd said thirteen when he didn't even flinch or hesitate.

"Done. Come see what I have in mind."

It occurred to her, then, he could bring her in the house and kill her dead and not a soul on earth would even know where she was. On the other hand, he didn't seem like the type who would enjoy killing someone dead, and she was pretty sure she could outrun him if she had misread the situation or his intention.

She needn't have worried. Despite the early hour, the house was like a small city, bustling with activity and workers, none who seemed very welcoming toward her. She tried not to let her mouth hang open at the luxuriousness of the furnishings and fixtures of the mansion they were passing through.

She could tell right away that the other members of the household staff were not at all happy she had circumvented the system. Mr. King's assistant's nose seemed particularly out of joint. James wrung his hands and talked about applications and security checks, but Mr. King waved a hand at him, as though he were a bothersome fly, which earned her a look of venom.

Of course later, looking at herself in the mirror of a bathroom that was the size of her whole living room at home, she reluctantly understood James's concern. She had a leaf in her hair from where she had gone through the shrubs. In contrast to the richness of the bathroom—could that be real gold on the faucets?—she could see how poor she looked. Her clothes had been clean but obviously worn, and the vinyl on the cheap sneakers she'd worn was cracking with age.

But here she was now, three days later, sitting in her grandfather's office, compiling the history of a family she had not been a part of.

It was way easier than she'd thought it would be. Her grandfather had boxes full of photographs. She had to try and figure out what chronological order they should come in. Some had dates and explanations on the back, others didn't. Sarah had to divide them up, so that in the end, each of his daughters would get a gift of a completed album of the high points of her life with her father. At some point, the best of the photos would have to be selected, but she was a long way from that place. Months, perhaps.

Given the generosity of her pay arrangement, that thought should have made her gleeful, but it didn't.

The work was easy, the emotional part not so. Sarah was fighting demons of jealousy and anger as she sifted through the privileged enclaves of her aunts' lives.

She wanted to hate her grandfather, and yet found she could not. The photos helped her to know him. She could see he had been a good father to his girls, devoted and loving though wildly overindulgent.

He was such a genuinely nice man, sweet and courteous. He never corrected her grammar or stared pointedly at her chewed-down fingernails like his secretary, James. He wasn't snooty about her clothes like the other household staff. A maid had snickered at her just this morning and had asked snidely if she shopped at the Goodwill store.

Which she did.

Thankfully, most of the staff avoided Mr. King's den like the plague. He kept it roasting hot in here, but for a girl who'd been cold and worried about power bills most of her life, that suited her just fine.

Sarah looked up from her study of the photos, the constant sorting into stacks and years, and saw him looking at her.

Nothing lecherous in that look. She had long since figured out that if he was a dirty old man, he would have made his move by now.

"What?" she asked, disconcerted by the sadness in his face.

He shook his head. "For a moment, I thought you were Brandy," he said, and his voice cracked.

Brandy, Jessie, Chelsea, she probably knew those girls better than they knew themselves by now.

He put his hand up to his face, and she saw his shoulders heave, knew he was crying.

And she knew why. He was dying. She should have guessed that earlier. That was why he was putting together these albums.

She didn't want to feel bad for him, but she did.

It seemed like it might be a good time to tell him who

she really was, but suddenly it seemed too scary. As if she were a liar, had lied her way through his door.

But that begged the question, did she ever plan to tell him?

If he had wanted to know about her, wouldn't he have answered her letter?

She'd never had it better than this. Twelve dollars an hour. Yesterday, he'd told her if she wanted to bring her swimsuit, now that the weather was getting warmer, she could use the pool after work. She didn't have a swimsuit but she planned to get one. She was going to swim in that pool after all. And she'd been invited!

He didn't yell at her or make demands. He didn't think the fact that she brought him coffee every now and then and that he paid her wages entitled him to pinch her ass.

But it was all going to end. Her moments in paradise would be fleeting. He would die, and she would be put out on the curb faster than a good dog treed a possum.

But of course she had always known that. Nothing good had ever lasted for a McKenzie. Maybe that curse had started when her grandmother had fallen in love with a man so determined to rise above his own humble beginnings that he had left people behind.

It was going to end, and she'd be back in some greasy spoon swilling the hogs.

While her aunts would swim in that pool, and ride those horses, and flit around the world and inherit all of this. Every single stick and stone.

It was that thought that made her slip the ashtray into her sweater pocket. It was small, solid silver, it had candies in it, that nobody ever seemed to notice or eat. It was engraved in the bottom with his name.

She tried to tell herself it was something to remember him by, that it was all she would ever get from him.

But it didn't feel right. In fact, she felt awful. McKenzies might not have the best blood. But thieves? Still, the ashtray was in her pocket when she left the estate that night and began her long trudge toward town.

After the third car carrying a member of the household staff passed her with no offer for a lift, she almost convinced herself that the small piece of silver in her pocket belonged to her.

Chapter Five

Brandy awoke with a start, disoriented. But slowly she became aware of two things—she had rarely felt so physically uncomfortable, and yet, almost in counterbalance, she was feeling a most delicious sense of emotional well-being.

Green Eggs and Ham was lying open on the floor. She was on her side and she had her arm curled protectively around the baby, who was pulled in tight against her. In her sleep, Becky purred and slurped. The baby had moved closer and closer into the shelter of Brandy's body until she felt as if they were melting together.

Brandy had managed to comb the baby's hair, kind of. It was now adorned with little pink ribbons that matched Becky's dress. Brandy knew she should get up, get the baby into pajamas, go to bed, somewhere. But where, his bed?

A hand touched her shoulder, and she gasped in surprise and then realized that was what had awakened her in the first place.

"Brandy."

His voice was soft, a graveled gentleness that tingled along the length of her spine.

She rolled over and looked at him, sleepily, with deep appreciation. His hand stayed on her shoulder, strong, sure, connecting her with the lovely idea that she knew things about Clint that no one else in the world knew.

In her father's world, Clint was seen as intimidating. He was a big man and every ounce of his muscular frame telegraphed pure physical power, but there was more than that. He carried himself with the certainty of a man who knew exactly how to use his strength when it was needed. There was something in those tawny lion eyes that signaled he was not a man who would be crossed, tested or lied to. To add to the faint menace of his physical presence, he had a reputation as the man with the razor-sharp judgment.

Her father relied on him because Clint had unerring instinct, a commodity that was rare and beyond price in the business world. Clint made decisions that were not for the fainthearted and he made them with no hesitation. He had an almost arrogant confidence in his own judgment. He was respected by most, feared by many. He was one of those powerful men who radiated his power, who wore it like a skin, who was comfortable in it.

But on rare occasions that aura that Clint wore around himself—as impenetrable as a rock cliff dripping with ice—cracked open just a hair.

His hand on her shoulder now, radiating heat and unconscious sensuality, reminded her of a moment a long, long time ago.

It had been her prom night. She'd been seventeen, and she had thought she was alone in the dark garden at the back of Kingsway. She'd been crying, tears staining the Prada gown that had cost a king's ransom, and that had failed, miserably, to produce the feeling she wanted. She wanted to be as beautiful as her sister Chelsea, who was four years younger. The amount of male attention Chelsea garnered was infuriating.

In the showroom trying on the dress, with the salespeople cooing around her, she had thought she could, like Chelsea, be so beautiful that a room would grow quiet when she entered it. She was going to leave her tomboy image behind!

Instead, when Brandy had put on the dress for her prom and regarded herself in the privacy of her bedroom, she felt stupid in it, as if she were pretending to be someone she was not. The gown was a shade of silver that made her complexion look sallow. There was not enough material in it to make a good-sized handkerchief, and she did not have Chelsea's panache, even though Chelsea was only thirteen! No, Brandy looked flat-chested and gauche, like a child who had found a trunk in the attic and had dressed up in her fancy best for a tea party with an imaginary queen.

To make matters worse, a hairdresser had come to the house for the occasion, and tortured her hair into some horrible upswept do that would not do at all!

She was pretty sure her "date" had asked her to the

prom not because he liked her at all, but because she was a King. His family was well-to-do, too, of course, but not quite in the same category as her family. He probably really had a crush on Chelsea, or wanted Jess to tutor him for his science final, or was looking for an in with her father to talk about old cars.

Brandy had been able to accept the fact he had probably not asked her out for her because she had a secret fantasy that when she did her big "reveal," his jaw was going to drop with appreciation and he was going to instantly forget all his less-than-stellar motivations for asking her to the prom in the first place.

Moments ago, looking in the mirror, she had come to the conclusion that she looked utterly ridiculous. She could normally count on her father to reassure her in moments like this, but Jake really hadn't understood the significance of the prom. She had wanted him to understand it was important without having to explain it, but he hadn't gotten the thousand hints she had laid, and now he was away on business.

So, Brandy had given the maid, Benita, tearful instructions to tell the boy, when he arrived, that she wasn't going, and she'd fled to the garden.

But suddenly she wasn't alone on the bench. Clint had materialized out of the darkness and his hand rested on her shoulder.

"Brandy?"

"Go away."

But he didn't. He slid onto the bench next to her. His tone was exquisitely gentle. "What's wrong?"

He usually sounded so stern and so standoffish that

she was caught by surprise, and she suddenly knew she could trust him with any of her secrets.

So, she told him her doubts about the dress and the boy, and he didn't say anything for the longest time.

"You know, Brandy," he finally said, "it's okay to be scared."

"I'm not scared," she said huffily. "I'm not scared of anything. You saw me put a horse over a six-foot jump last week. I've done fifteen skydives!"

He was silent for a time, and then he said very, very quietly, "We're all scared of the very same things, Brandy. Of not fitting, of not belonging, of not being liked for who we really are."

She took a sharp breath at that accurate assessment of her situation, but then realized that was exactly what he was known for—seeing through all the facades to the truth underneath.

"Just go and be yourself," he advised. "And everything will be okay."

She was seventeen! She didn't have a clue who she was!

And then he handed her a shawl, a beautiful antique ivory shawl of the most delicate lace. As soon as she put it over her shoulders, she knew that it toned down the dress, turning it from something that was way over the top into something just about perfect.

"How did you know this would fix the dress?" she said, getting up from the bench and twirling in front of him with the shawl. "Men don't know things like that."

"I saw you come down the stairs. I asked Benita to find something so that it wasn't quite so, er, revealing. She says the shawl was your mother's."

Brandy's memories of her mother were faint and not altogether pleasant. Her mother had disapproved of rambunctiousness, blue jeans and dirt, though from all reports, her fashion sense had been unquestionable.

"One more thing."

He took the pins from her coiffed hair, tousled it with his hands. She stood, frozen under his touch, wishing suddenly that everything were different.

"That's better," he said with a faint smile.

Oh, how she wished that she were older. Or that he were younger. That she could just sit here with him, in the darkness, feeling this way: hopeful, accepted, excited, as if the very air tingled with possibility, though she was not even sure for what.

They heard the front door chime and suddenly everything felt different than it had only three minutes ago. She hurried away before the maid sent the boy away when now she wanted to go to her prom after all.

But then she turned back. She needed to know something. She needed to know it badly enough that if the boy got sent away, he got sent away.

"Clint?"

"Hmm?"

"You're not scared, are you? Of not being liked for who you really are?"

He snorted softly.

"Are you?" she pressed.

He sighed, hesitated, and then gave her the gift she needed most, his absolute honesty. "Look around you, Brandy. It's a big fairy tale, and I'm a boy from the bad side of the tracks. Not a day goes by when I don't think somebody's going to realize that and send me back to where I belong."

"Clint—" She started to go back toward him. Really, hearing the fascinating details of a youth that sounded like it had been wildly misspent sounded much more intriguing than going to the prom with Tommy Wilson.

But Clint got up from the bench and stood regarding her, his hands deep in his pockets, that more familiar expression of cynicism on his face.

Even though she was young, she knew intuitively that he regretted saying those words about himself, that moment of vulnerability.

"Go on," he said, a harsh rasp to his voice. "Have fun."

Long after the prom, which had been far more forgettable than the events that preceded it, Brandy fantasized about pursuing that little tidbit he'd tossed out almost carelessly that night. But the opportunity never presented itself. He never allowed it to present itself again. Clint was always the perfect gentleman, polite, but faintly distant. Respectful, but not familiar; friendly, but not inviting confidence.

And she had allowed herself to be intimidated by the presence he exuded until the night of her nineteenth birthday party. This time, the gown, designed specifically for her by Giorgio Armani, had fit her perfectly. And this time, bolstered by one too many glasses of champagne, she'd—

No! She was not thinking of that, her most embarrassing moment.

Instead, she drew herself back to the here and now, lying on the floor of his living room, with Clint's hand on her shoulder. She banished her memories of *that* night and allowed the lovely sensation of warmth to spread farther.

He was kneeling on the rug, leaning over her. Despite a fishing vest, decorated with hooks and suspicious-looking stains, Clint looked gorgeous. The dark silk of his hair was falling carelessly over his brow, the sharp planes of his face were whisker-roughened, and his eyes were dark. His pupils huge in the dim room, rimmed with an exquisite ring of pure gold.

Dreamily, still half-asleep, lost in the sensation of that memory and the pure contentment that was sweeping over her, she reached up and did something she had always dreamed of doing. She scraped her palm across the whisker-roughness of that cheek, touched the fullness of his lower lip with her thumb.

His intake of breath was sharp, but he did not pull away. She held her own breath, waiting to see if he would accept this invitation, nuzzle her thumb. Though he did not pull away from her touch, he returned nothing.

The sensation of his lip, faintly damp, full, as sensuous as cold silk on a warm night, was so exquisite she had to close her eyes against it. She was totally unsure what she was experiencing, heaven or hell.

Because alarm bells were going off in her, trying to remind her of something. Finally it did pierce the hazy wall of sensation she was feeling. Hadn't she come here to prove something? That she was all grown-up and mature and that she had left that childhood crush for him so far behind her that the memory couldn't sting anymore?

Yet in this one moment, she knew she was farther from her goal, rather than closer.

The child beside her sputtered and mewed, and she knew the baby complicated everything, including the way her heart felt.

Tender.

And tender things bruised so easily.

She drew her hand away hastily. "Sorry," she muttered and sat up on her elbows. "I'm partly asleep."

"Did you mistake me for someone else?" He looked chagrined, and she might have been foolish enough to wonder if that meant she should hope he could like her in *that way*, but instead she remembered his reaction to the boy who had delivered the trampoline.

He was simply protective, nothing personal, part of that fierce warrior makeup of his.

"Yes," she lied. "I mistook you for someone else." As if *he* could be mistaken for someone else.

He looked like he knew she was lying. Now he would think she *wanted* to touch his lips and his face, which she did, but it would be so much easier if he didn't know.

She carefully untangled herself from the baby, struggled to sitting, rubbed at her eyes and ran a hand through her hair. She was still in his shirt, but she had thrown on a pair of his sweatpants against the chill of the evening. They were about ten sizes too large for her, and she had the sneaking suspicion she looked like a scarecrow. What else was new?

"Is my makeup running?" she demanded.

She took his shrug as a yes.

"I can't believe we fell asleep here. I was going to read Becky a story, and then put her to bed, but somehow…"

Her voice trailed off.

A terrible realization hit her as she sat there on the rug. She could smell the sweet tang of him, and she wanted only to taste his lips, to touch the broadness of his chest, to feel the steel of his thigh against her own. She wanted him with a savage longing that was quite unlike anything she had ever felt before. And if that longing had been strictly physical, it would not have made her feel panicky, the way she felt now.

She loved him. She had loved him always and she loved him still.

She leaped to her feet, hauled the too-large sweatpants up so that the crotch wasn't quite at her knees, and looked around wildly.

"I didn't get around to dinner," she confessed, looking for something to say that would hide what she had just discovered from those golden eyes that always saw everything. "I planned to, but it's impossible. Have you ever tried to get takeout delivered here? I've never been hung up on so many times in my life!"

"Don't worry about dinner."

"Oh, I'm not," she said breezily, though of course she was. Because she wanted him to think highly of her and care about her and love her back.

And she could see she would make a complete fool of herself if she stayed here, trying to make that happen.

The feelings inside of her were just way too intense. She felt as if she were walking a tightrope, and if she fell one way she would know pain greater than anything she had ever known, and if she fell the other she would know the same extreme of pleasure.

Only she didn't feel as if she were going to have any control over which side of that tightrope she landed on.

No, it was all going to be up to him. If he returned even the smallest measure of what she felt for him, then it would be the pleasure side, but if he didn't, if he rejected her all over again, she would get to experience misery so intense it drove people to leap off high buildings—some without the benefit of a puny little rip cord.

"I have to leave," she said, and hoped he could not hear the faint note of desperation in her voice.

"Leave?" he said, frowning.

"Yes, leave. Right now."

"You mean go to your cabin for the night?"

"No! I have to leave—" *you* "—here."

"Tonight?" he asked, astounded.

Tonight would be good. Impossible, unless she left all her stuff behind, and then he might *know*.

"No, first thing in the morning, though. I've had a call from Jason."

"Ah," he said, rocking back on his heels and folding his arms over the massiveness of his chest, regarding her with faint disbelief. "And Jason is?"

"A friend. A good friend. The boy who's asked me to marry him, actually."

She knew as soon as she blurted it out how wrong it sounded, but he picked up on the part of it that was wrong.

"A boy," he said, with the softest edge of scorn.

And she knew it was true. Jason was a boy. Immature and self-centered, perhaps even colossally so. They'd been friends for years, and none of those things had mattered, as long as they were just friends.

Then the mistake had happened. After years of being pals, in a moment that was probably inspired by a touch too much champagne, Jason had seen her romantically. His great wonder in discovering his best buddy was actually a girl had lasted for all of two weeks.

Then, without a word of warning, he'd disappeared, and suddenly he'd been in the newspapers squiring Ivory Cuthbert, heiress to the Cuthbert newspaper fortune. Then, again without warning, he'd been back, on his knees, claiming to have seen the light. Wanting marriage. Wanting only her, Brandy King, for the rest of his life.

She had said she needed time to think things over, but her time with Clint was not helping her sort through anything. It just confused everything more.

Only one thing was crystal clear: Clint was a man. Jason was a boy.

But they did have something in common. They had both rejected her, as surely as her mother had when she was a tot.

Wasn't that really her greatest fear in the world? The fear of being rejected? All those years ago, when she had hooked up with Jason and his crowd, hadn't that been part of the appeal? Acceptance was easy to guarantee: you just had to jump into the embrace of air, canoe a bit of white water, dig crampons deep into ice. You had to be wild and crazy and rich. In other words, the price of playing poker was low, not a whole lot was required of her at all.

And Clint seemed to know that with that terrible intuition of his! Brandy tossed her head in the face of Clint's scorn, lifted her chin. "Jason's got something spectacular planned. He's been scouting the next location. He said something about Baffin Island. A five-thousand-foot cliff. I'll have to go."

Clint's expression went from cynical to dazed, as if he had been hit hard and unexpectedly from behind.

"Not that I haven't enjoyed it here," she rushed on. "It's been great. A regular slice of normal life. A baby. Laundry. I'd be a riot on a reality series. Me and Paris Hilton. Not that all this domestic stuff is my cup of tea, but it's been educational."

"What happened to laundry being fun?" he asked her, standing up.

He looked down at her, and she had that awful feeling she had around him sometimes—most of the time—that nothing could be hidden from him, those eyes fastened on her face with that wicked, *knowing* intelligence.

She had that awful feeling of being way too aware of him as a man. Of the way her curves would fit perfectly against the hard sculpture of his masculinity…

"I did a few more loads," she said, her voice way too rushed and breathless for a simple discussion about laundry. She shrugged, with deliberate carelessness, an effort to counteract any secrets her voice was giving away. "The novelty wore off."

"So, some guy who claims to love you wants you to jump off a cliff with him, and you're going to go?"

She hated how he said that. "Like nobody could really love me?" she snapped.

"I don't think anybody who really cared about you would be encouraging reckless, foolhardy behavior."

"Jason and I are cut from the same cloth."

"Dear God, that's downright frightening."

She shrugged again, even more carelessly than before, but she was stung. Nothing he could do or say could make her stay here, now. She was not going to be insulted. Judged. Treated like an idiot child.

He took a deep breath. He looked like he wanted to shake her until her teeth rattled, so when he took her shoulders in his hands, she braced herself.

That familiar dangerous current hummed to life between them, and he did not shake her. He looked at her long and hard, and suddenly, the light in his eyes softened.

He looked at her lips and licked his own.

She remembered how his lips had felt under the touch of her thumb, only moments ago. She held her breath. If he kissed her, what would she do?

Kiss him back, of course.

But what would the repercussions be? What would it mean?

She needn't have worried because he did not kiss her.

"No, Brandy, you can't go."

She felt herself getting defensive all over again. She wasn't a child anymore, who could be bossed around. She couldn't allow him to intimidate her. Give her orders.

But her sharp reply caught in her throat, unspoken, when he said so softly she almost couldn't hear him, "I need you."

Her mouth fell open. She was pretty sure her vision was blurring. Were those tears? God, how embarrassing!

Was she swooning, because damn, hearing those words was almost as good as being kissed. Maybe even better.

He needed her?

Clint McPherson needed Brandy King?

It seemed her whole life she had waited for that, for someone somewhere to need her. She was not strong enough to walk away from that. Not yet.

What had happened to nothing he could do or say would make her stay here now? It had been a lie, she realized, just like so many others she had told herself.

Jeez, Clint wondered to himself, did anything with this woman ever go according to plan? His plan, that was?

He had marched up to this house, rehearsing his dismissal speech. For his sanity, Brandy had to go, no ifs, ands or buts.

Except there was a but and it was this: in light of what she planned to go to, some silly young pup named Jason and a trip to a five-thousand-foot cliff on Baffin Island, saving his own sanity, keeping his world carefully controlled seemed paltry and self-centered.

This was probably why her father had sent her here, to keep her out of harm's way.

Clint wasn't letting her go jump off the top of a waterfall somewhere because she was scared to death of what had just passed between them when her hand had grazed his cheek.

Okay, it had been scary. It had taken every ounce of his willpower not to nibble that delectable thumb that had explored his lip with such tentative boldness. It had underscored his absolute knowing that she had to go.

But he was going to have to put his own need to get rid of her on hold until this threat to her safety passed.

What if something happened to her because of him, because he was afraid of what a little chit of a girl could do to his heart?

And she did look like a little chit, right now, still dressed in his shirt, a pair of sweatpants that he was pretty sure belonged to him, too, absolutely swimming around her. Her hair was a mess, and she did have dark makeup smudges under her eyes, not to mention a little pattern on her cheek where it had been pressed into the rug.

Really, the picture she made should have been funny. Absurd. Rebecca had never had a hair out of place, not even in the morning when she'd woken up. She had always worn tailored silk, even to bed.

So, how was it that Brandy in this getup looked as sexy as any woman he had ever seen?

He was just going to have to be more disciplined.

"You need me?" she whispered.

Especially if she was going to use that tone of voice on him!

"No," she said, before he could answer, "that can't be right. I don't even know how to change a diaper."

"You do now," he reminded her, and felt guilty. He was manipulating her. It was wrong. But if it kept her from extreme foolishness, then was it right?

"Or run the thing that washes clothes. What are they called again?"

"The washing machine," he told her drily. "That apparatus that you've used a zillion times."

A ghost of a smile. "I knew that. I would have remembered that." She looked at his face, and she was trying hard to see truth. "Look, I know you are about the most self-sufficient guy ever born, so I'll just pack up my stuff and go in the morning. You don't need me."

"It's not all about me," he said, suddenly as desperate to keep her here as he had been to get rid of her when he had docked that boat fifteen minutes ago. "It's about her."

Brandy glanced at the baby.

"Out on the boat, I realized I'm worn out. I need a break every now and then."

She looked skeptical.

"And she needs a feminine influence. Look at the dress and the little ribbons in her hair. I've never done that. The poor kid hasn't been out of sleepers in three months."

Brandy looked at the baby, and the expression on her face of unguarded tenderness nearly slew him.

It reminded him how weak he could be around her, how quickly everything could spin out of control. His control. He felt again that niggle of guilt for manipulating her, even if it was for her own good.

"I guess I could stay for a little while. Just to help a bit around here. Until you find a nanny or something. I could probably help you find a nanny."

"Thanks, Brandy."

She took a step toward him, lifted her hand. For a frozen, terrifying moment, he thought she was going to touch his lip again, and there was only so much a man—even one with a legendary amount of discipline—could withstand.

Her hand dropped abruptly and her cheeks flooded with color. Her tone, when she spoke, was flip.

"Hey, Sober-sides, no problem. I'll help you out for a while. But right now, I gotta go to bed. See you in the morning. Oh, the rest of the laundry I did is on your bed." She sounded proud and shy, too.

"Uh, thanks."

"See you in the morning." But she didn't move. She ducked her head, tucked a strand of hair behind her ear and then looked back at him.

"You need me?" she whispered. "Seriously?"

For a guy who was supposed to be some kind of expert on people, he saw a stunning truth about her.

She had never been needed.

Wasn't it one of the most basic human desires? To be needed? To have a purpose? To belong?

He, on the other hand, had rarely not been needed. Often his younger brother Cameron's very survival had seemed to depend on Clint's ability to read the mood in their far-too-volatile house. And then along had come Jake King, who had needed Clint's peculiar gifts. Now his tiny daughter needed him with a dependency so great it sometimes felt as if the weight of the whole world rode solely on his shoulders.

"Yeah," he said gruffly, "I need you."

Brandy stared at him, smiled a secretive, touching little smile and then turned away. There was a little spring in her step as she moved across the floor and out the back door. She paused and gave him a little wave.

He went to the window and watched as she sashayed down the pathway and across the lawn to her little cabin, leaving him feeling like a man who had just been hit by something, but who wasn't quite sure what.

He scooped up the sleeping baby, who barely stirred. In the nursery, Clint managed to get Becky out of the crushed dress and into her pj's. He was not sure where the dress had come from. It had probably been a gift that he had taken one look at, been terrified by the delicacy of it in his big hands, and had stuffed into the back of a drawer.

He also didn't know where the ribbon had come from. He counted eight pink bows tied in the hopeless tangle of his daughter's hair. He didn't know if ribbon was a choking hazard, but he wasn't taking any chances, so he clumsily removed each of them. Little, tiny ribbons were hard for big, male hands, a hazard just like little frou-frou dresses! Finally, he laid her down, touched her forehead with his hand, bent and kissed her.

He went through the adjoining door to his room.

His bed was covered with untidy stacks of clothing, badly folded. His socks and undershirts had a suspicious pink tinge to them. Three of his favorite golf sweaters were laid out side by side. They looked like they would fit Becky when she turned three or four. His jeans had been leached of color in wild patterns that reminded him of pictures he had seen of hippies in the sixties.

Despite the wreckage, all he could think was that Brandy had been in here, had invaded his masculine sanctuary, and that it was quite possible the ghost of her presence was going to linger there for all time.

He hoped she'd had the decency to stay out of his drawers—every kind he owned—but he doubted it.

He sighed and swept the piles of clothing onto the floor, crawled into his bed, and became aware of the faintest little smile tickling his lips.

"It's not a smiling matter," he told himself. "You told her you needed her." From the look on her face, it had been the message she had been waiting her entire life to hear.

He had the feeling she would attack being needed with her customary vengeance.

But, at least she wouldn't be jumping off cliffs in the Far North or engaging in other activities equally heart-stopping.

A man had to do what a man had to do.

In that vulnerable moment before sleep, when unwanted thoughts crept past a man's guard, this thought came to him.

His life had been washed in a gray pallor, until she had come.

She was like glimpsing the sun through heavy fog.

Was it possible that he did need Brandy King in ways he had not begun to acknowledge?

"I certainly hope not," he groaned out loud.

Chapter Six

Brandy awoke at 5:00 a.m. so excited, so bursting with ideas about how to help Clint, that she couldn't go back to sleep. The birds were singing with glorious joy outside her window, and when she looked out, the sun was already splashing merrily across the lake and the flower beds.

She wasn't sure when she had last awoken so aware of the wonders of the world around her, feeling such a great sense of wellbeing and hope for the day. Had she ever felt like this? No, not even when Jason and the gang were planning something *big*. That definition of *big* now seemed exceedingly childish, as if it were something she had been waiting to outgrow.

She scribbled herself a little list of to-dos and realized she needed both Internet access and a coffee, and neither were available here in her little cottage. She showered and dressed, and despite her eagerness to get on with her day, she took a bit more time with her appearance than normal.

She scooped up her hair in a clip, found a pair of jeans that were just a little too tight and a wildly colored blouse with belled arms and a plunging neckline that was distinctly more girlish than what she generally wore. In her own defense, she had to erase the scarecrow outfit of yesterday from a certain man's mind. She dusted on a bit of makeup—just enough to make her eyes look huge and sapphire and to make her lips look luscious and inviting—and finished with a breath of perfume behind each ear.

Then Brandy grabbed her laptop and headed to the main house. There was a small built-in desk in the kitchen and soon she was totally engrossed in her search for ways, not just to help him, but to brighten his boring existence immeasurably.

She was so engrossed that she nearly jumped out of her skin when he cleared his throat. She turned in her chair, and her breath caught.

The fact that he wasn't expecting her to be in his kitchen this early was evident. Clint was leaning in the doorjamb of the kitchen, eyeing her warily. The early morning sun was streaming in from a window behind him and outlined him in light that made his skin seem to shimmer bronze. And there was quite a lot of skin, as Clint was wearing a pair of plaid pajama trousers that hung dangerously low on his hips and nothing else.

She had known he was an exquisitely made man, mus-cled and lean, but nothing had prepared her for the naked reality of him. He was absolute perfection, an artist's dream, his body perfectly proportioned, an unconscious power and grace flowing through every line of him.

Her eyes drank in the low cut of those pajama trousers, how his hip bones jutted above them and his belly stretched taut and hard-muscled between his hips. He had what the kids in her crowd called a six-pack, sculptured ridges on his belly rising to his ribs.

How on earth could he look like this? He was *old*.

But his body was not old; in fact, she appreciated the maturity of it. He had none of the greyhound leanness of youth, but all the solidness of a man who had come fully into his strength. That picture of strength was completed as her eyes roved up to his chest, broad, perfectly mounded pecs, brazenly masculine.

"Do you work out?" she asked him, and her voice was an embarrassing croak.

"Sometimes. There's a gym in the basement." Something flashed in his eyes, and she knew he was not immune to feminine appreciation of his very masculine body. She also knew he had taken in her sexy blouse and stretch jeans with appreciation of his own.

If she got up, went to him, placed the coolness of her palm on the flatness of that belly, what would he do?

Would he trace a finger lightly, teasingly, over her décolleté? Would he ravage her lips? His eyes said maybe. But the stern downturn of his mouth spoke of another possibility. That he would jerk away from her, retreat to his room, reappear hours or days later buttoned up to the throat.

Brandy wanted to take risks of the kind she had not

taken before—risks with her heart—but she was not entirely sure she could deal with rejection.

So, fighting back the temptation to explore that *thing* that tingled in the air between them, she turned back to her computer, but not before finishing a quick inventory of his tousled hair, not before she noted that whisker-roughness of his face yesterday had deepened into dark bronze shadows. And not before she noticed that his feet were bare. There was something extremely sexy about a man in bare feet, though she had to admit she was twenty-six years old and she had never, ever noticed that before.

"What are you doing up so early?" he asked, not moving from the kitchen doorway, getting ready to bolt for that button-down shirt if he had to.

"I just thought I'd get an early start on the day." She returned her attention to the laptop and pretended to study it intently. It took a great deal of willpower to keep her eyes on the screen instead of drinking in the picture he made.

"I think the coffee's ready," she said. She could tell he was on the verge of turning around and going to get dressed, but she thought the lure of the brew might postpone that moment.

Besides, she was very pleased about the coffee, though she hadn't sampled it yet. Of course she knew how to make coffee! Okay, so the kind of coffeemaker she was accustomed to came with premeasured pouches and his didn't, but she still was fairly confident, from the heavenly aroma in the room, that she had gotten it just right.

She watched out of the corner of her eye as he padded

across the floor, reached up to the cupboard for his favorite mug, poured coffee.

No one had warned her that a half-naked man in the morning was pure poetry to watch—every unconscious stretch and flex of muscle entrancing. He rested his behind against the countertop, took a sip of the coffee—and winced.

Too strong, she guessed sadly. "Is it bad?" she asked.

"No, no. Just the jolt I needed." Ever the gentleman, he took another manly sip just to prove it, and then he wandered over behind her and peered over her shoulder. "What are you doing?"

For a moment, she forgot exactly what she was doing, because she felt his breath on her neck, heard him inhale her scent, sigh.

Exasperated that this feminine temptation was in his world? Or reluctantly appreciative of her presence?

She glanced over her shoulder at him.

He was squinting at her open screen, the scowl lines deepening along his forehead. She realized, distracting scents aside, he might not approve of her Internet research. She pressed Exit so that her screen saver came up.

He swore softly, and she realized he didn't approve of that, either.

The screen saver was of her guiding her canopy to a perfect landing at the base of Angel Falls.

"It's not as dangerous as it looks," she said. "I'm very careful."

"Humph." He shifted his weight restlessly. She could smell coffee and the wonderful, heady, clean-sheet scent of a man still tousled from sleep.

Before she realized what he intended, he had reached over her shoulder and restored the previous screen she'd been looking at.

"I wonder what you were so eager to hide?" he mused.

"I wasn't hiding anything," she said, but she knew she might as well have saved her breath. Clint could just look at people and know if they were hiding something.

Did he have any idea that she was hiding the greatest secret of all?

That she loved him?

She glanced at his face. No, even Clint could be trusted to be a true man in that area. Obtuse until the end.

"Lucky Little Lucy," he read out loud. "A Welsh pony out of Little Lucky Herbert and Lucy's Lace. Offered at nine thousand British pounds sterling. Shipping extra."

Brandy watched him hopefully as he studied the pony in the picture. Lucy was adorable with her burnished gold coat and her white mane and tail, the mane nearly touching the ground the pony was so small. Who could resist her?

"Are you kidding?" he asked incredulously.

Apparently he could!

"She's so cute and tiny, Clint. You'd hardly even know she was here."

"Ha! Becky's tiny and cute, too. There's no missing her. No pony."

"What do you mean, no?" she said, a trifle stunned. People did not say no to her in that tone of voice. People rarely said no to her at all!

"I have enough on my plate, thanks."

"I'll look after it."

"Yeah. For a week or two."

That really brought forward the issue neither of them had discussed. How long was she staying?

Her heart was very foolishly saying forever. And if it wasn't forever, she was leaving Becky something to remember her by! She didn't care what he said.

"You know what? I recognize that mutinous look on your face. I know exactly what you are up to, and let me put the kibosh on it before you get too far. You are not getting a pony for Becky. Don't even think about sneaking Little Miss Lucky—"

"Lucy," she corrected him.

"In here behind my back. Becky does not need a pony. Good grief, Brandy, in case you haven't noticed, she can't even walk yet."

"I know, but haven't you ever heard the expression about riding before walking? It's true! Her comfort level with horses will be wonderful if we can introduce her to them now. And the benefits of balance—"

She noticed she had said *we*. Apparently he hadn't noticed, or he'd decided to ignore it.

He cut her off, with a groan, before she could name any of the benefits of developing balance at a tender age. "I should have never given in on the trampoline." He took a rather large swig of the coffee and winced again.

"You don't have to pretend you like the coffee," she said coolly, miffed completely that he had caught her before she had managed to order the pony. If she could have gotten it here, he would have found it irresistible. And even if he hadn't found it irresistible, he wouldn't have been mean enough to send Lucy away once Becky had seen her.

"All right, I won't pretend to like the coffee." Apparently he was just a little miffed himself, if the way he slammed down the mug on the desktop beside her was any indication. "No pony."

"Clint, just think about it. You have all that grass out there."

"I like to think of it as a lawn, not a pasture. I can't see that it would be improved by little mounds of horse poop."

"Horse poop is good fertilizer. Think of your precious flower garden."

"Believe me, I am. I can tell by looking at that horse, she'd eat my flowers."

"You can tell that by looking at her?" Brandy demanded.

"She has the beady little eyes of a begonia fiend."

"That's ridiculous." Brandy wasn't quite sure what a begonia was, but surely whatever it was, it couldn't be more important than a pony for his daughter.

"You know what is ridiculous? That we are even having this conversation. No pony. That's the end of it."

Brandy was not accustomed to being told that was the end of anything, and yet when she glanced into his face, she shivered. It would be foolhardy to pursue this—right now. Maybe later, when he was in a more mellow mood. After she'd proven how helpful she could be, a tiny pony would seem like nothing.

Still, just to prove to him he was an utterly ridiculous man, she got up and got herself a cup of coffee.

She took a deep sip and schooled herself not to wince.

It was harder than she had thought it would be. The coffee was dreadful!

He wasn't watching her anyway. He had slipped into the chair at the built-in desk and was looking at her laptop.

She forced herself to make a deep satisfied *ahh* sound over the coffee. He glanced at her and grinned wickedly, not the least bit fooled. She took another deep, defiant sip, but she might as well have saved herself.

He wasn't paying the least bit of attention to her. He had her Internet history open and was scanning it with interest.

"Let's see what else you've been up to this morning," he said.

"That's private!"

"Well, so is my underwear drawer, but that didn't stop you."

"I was putting away laundry." Okay, curiosity had gotten the better of her. The starched white boxers shouldn't have surprised her one little bit.

"The Alabama Fireworks Company?" he muttered.

"The Fourth of July is coming! I thought a little show on the front lawn—"

"No," he said, and hit the delete button. "I like my lawn. No horse nuggets. No scorch marks. No forest fires, come to that. This part of the world has been mercifully free of excitement since the war of 1812."

She glared at the back of his head. "I wouldn't burn up your lawn with a few little fireworks. Or the stupid forest. And a little excitement is not always a bad thing."

Unfortunately, that made her think of touching his bare chest again!

But he only snorted, completely unaware that her mind was very naughtily thinking of all kinds of excitement that had not a thing to do with fireworks.

He scanned down her history. "And no to Clowns-for-Hire." Delete. "And no to Chinese food from the Hoy Ping in New York. Were you going to fly it in? Seriously?"

At her small, stiff nod, he hit the delete button with what seemed to be an inordinate amount of pleasure.

"It was going to be a surprise," she said mutinously.

"Well, there. The surprise is wrecked, so don't bother."

"Believe me, I won't. Have you ever heard the expression about wasting your pearls on swine?"

"Actually, that isn't even close to the expression, which is biblical. Still, are you suggesting I'm a swine? Tut-tut. You'll hurt my feelings."

"If you had any," she muttered.

"Exactly. Now, what is this?" He was perusing her Internet history with an evil eye. "An online clothing store for toddlers. Haute Tot. Hot Tot meet Little Miss Lucky in the reject pile."

"Wait! Don't delete that."

His hand hovered.

"Let me show you." She abandoned her coffee, shoved him over on the chair and sat down beside him.

A mistake, since he was nearly naked and she could feel the wonder of his skin way too close to hers. His thigh and hers were touching. Everything seemed to intensify, the light in the room, the delightful aroma coming off him, the beat of her heart. Brandy pretended to be focusing exclusively on the screen.

So did he.

"Watch this," she said as the site opened.

He folded his arms over his chest and tapped his

foot. She clicked on a bar that she had created previously that said Baby Becky.

"I put in everything about her—her weight and her height and her hair color and hairstyle."

"She doesn't have a hairstyle," he muttered. "And twenty-two inches is a height?"

She ignored his cynicism. "And voilà, look—a virtual baby."

She could feel the subtle shift in him when a computer-generated picture of a baby that looked remarkably like Becky appeared on the screen. He uncrossed his arms and leaned forward. His foot quit tapping.

"Now watch," Brandy said. The computer baby was dressed in an undershirt and diapers. On the left side of the screen was a border with a selection of a dozen outfits. Brandy selected a particularly cute one, a bright red hooded jacket with matching pants. The jacket and pants both featured rolled-up cuffs in a contrasting material with bright printed dinosaurs on them. She clicked the outfit.

The outfit was immediately put on the virtual baby. As a finishing touch, she clicked on a pair of red socks with pom-poms and a tiny pair of red running shoes.

Clint's mouth dropped open. For a moment, he sat in stunned silence and then he reached for the mouse. "Hey, let me do that."

He selected a different outfit from the border—a little denim dress—and clicked. Catching on quickly, he added a pair of matching shoes and even a little hair ornament.

The virtual baby beamed out at him, and Clint laughed out loud.

Gone completely were the sternness and cynicism. She glanced at his face and saw how young he looked when he relaxed. Young and exceedingly, heart-stoppingly good-looking.

Finally, she had gotten something right! Or wrong, depending on how she wanted to look at it. She was sharing a chair with the most glorious man ever made by God. His leg was touching hers. He was laughing. It was a moment that a person could wish to go on forever and ever.

There was that word again, *forever.*

It was the second time in less than an hour it had crossed her mind. She was going to have to be bold in a different way than she had ever been bold before. She was going to have to find out if forever was even a possibility with Clint.

Or if he would hit the delete button on that idea as ruthlessly as he had on some of the others she had presented him with this morning.

"Are you telling me I can shop like this?" he asked Brandy, unaware apparently of all the undercurrents that she was feeling.

"Yes," she managed to choke out.

"My God, girl, you are a genius."

She had to find the courage within herself—real courage—to embrace the myriad emotions within her and then to see if he was ready to embrace it, too.

The thought was so frightening that for a moment she actually felt faint.

"Brandy, are you okay?"

"Oh, sure. Just contemplating the fact I've finally been recognized. A genius. Now about that pony."

She would play it light, for now. Obviously she could not just spring it on him, before breakfast, that she was in love with him. She would have to build up to it, set the scene. What about if she prepared a romantic candlelight dinner? She didn't exactly know how to do that, but she was sure she could find someone who did.

Her mind went to the hot tub outside. She would cook him dinner, pop a bottle of wine, get him in the hot tub. No, maybe not the wine. She didn't want any shades of her nineteenth birthday ruining this second declaration of love.

How would she do it? Kiss him. See if he kissed her back. And if he did...

He was blissfully unaware of the web that she was weaving around him. "I cannot tell you how terrifying it is for a man to go into the baby department looking for anything. If I take Becky with me, it's worse. I'm swarmed by women cooing and talking baby talk. It's truly awful."

"I'm sure being swarmed by women is truly awful," she said, trying not to feel jealous and not succeeding.

"Well, it is."

She slid him a look and realized he was serious. It said a lot about him. He was a man of deep integrity who would never play on his own good looks or the drawing appeal of his baby to take advantage of women who were obviously quite eager to be taken advantage of. He was a serious man who did not take anything lightly.

The jealousy evaporated in her, an emotion not worthy of the largeness of what she was beginning to feel.

Clint was far too serious, she decided, and she was, too. She would not miss this moment he was giving her like an unexpected gift because she was plotting for future ones! Brandy deliberately pushed a button that put a little purple joker's hat on the virtual baby's head.

The result was just what she wanted. Clint laughed out loud, again, and so did she.

The tension dissolved in her as, side by side, they took turns picking outfits off the virtual rack and trying them on the virtual baby. Laughing over an outlandish hat, arguing amiably about the suitability of a fancy party dress she wanted and the denim boys' overalls that he selected, they went through nearly every single outfit Haute Tot had to offer.

Given their differences, their tastes for the baby were remarkably similar—they both liked bold primary colors and clothing styles that were made for real playing, not for posing for pictures. They spent a delicious hour together filling the shopping basket with summer clothes, swimsuits, sun bonnets, the party dress and the overalls.

"Now," Brandy said, "how about the Dockers site for you?"

"No, thanks. I'm shopped out for today."

"I thought you needed me," she teased. "I thought you wanted my help!"

"I think we should define what I meant by that. Right now what it means is you go get the baby up, and I'll rustle up some breakfast."

"Is she going to be stinky?"

"Hopefully."

"How about," she said brightly, "if I make the breakfast and you go get the baby up?"

"Not if your coffee is any indication of the damage you can do in the kitchen."

"I bet I could have breakfast flown in for the right price."

"I bet you could, too, but how about if you don't?"

"Okay," she surrendered, laughing, "I'll do baby duty."

Becky was awake, happy in her crib, wagging her feet at the ceiling. She needed a fresh diaper, but the one that had to be changed was not of the stinky variety.

While Brandy shoved wildly waving limbs into fresh sleepers, she told the baby about the new wardrobe coming.

The baby reached out and touched her nose.

"Ba-ba?" she said experimentally.

Brandy's heart stopped. Was the baby trying to say her name?

She pointed at herself. "Ba-ba?" she asked.

The baby squealed with delight. "Ba-ba," she agreed.

Brandy's heart swelled within her chest. Oh, this was a dangerous game she was playing, getting in deeper and deeper. Her plan, to clarify things, was perfect.

After tonight, she would know.

Whether to stay, or whether to go, whether to give her heart wings, or whether to clip them.

She took a deep breath.

Maybe, for once, she was embracing a real risk. The risk of losing, not her life, but her heart.

Still, what if today was her last day with this beautiful baby? Would she hold back from her, or give her everything she had to give? The answer was obvious. Brandy picked up the baby, kissed her curly head and whispered, "That's right, sweetheart, ba-ba. That's me. Ba-ba."

She came into the kitchen. Normally Clint just put out a selection of cereals and made the baby some pablum, but this morning the kitchen smelled of frying bacon and pancakes. Apparently he had either forgotten his state of undress, or was quite comfortable with it, because he was still in the plaid pajama bottoms and nothing else.

Brandy got the baby settled in her high chair with a bottle that she microwaved carefully according to yesterday's instructions. Then she sidled over, ostentatiously to help, but she knew it was about being close to him. She was aware now of things he was not aware of. That they were arriving at a crossroads.

That this might be her last day here.

Or it might be the first day of the rest of her life.

"You know how to cook pancakes?" he asked. A mundane question for such a monumental day, but she was glad for it. Glad that no matter what happened, she was having this moment.

"Oh, sure," she said. "You know. Zillions of times."

The moment seemed suffused with a strange, dancing light. It was a moment free from the discontent that had plagued her entire life.

A moment when she felt strangely full instead of empty.

He laughed and handed her a flipper. "Even though you've done it a zillion times, remember to wait for the holes to appear in this side."

It was a silly thing, watching for those holes, feeling such a strong desire to get it exactly right, as if it mattered somehow more than anything she had ever done before.

And maybe it did. Being here with this makeshift family cooking breakfast gave her a glimpse of the one thing she had never, ever had.

Normal.

The baby slurped milk in the background and strained to get a better look at her chubby toes, singing her new mantra of ba-ba all the time.

"Is that a new word?" Clint asked. "Ouch." The grease kept spattering up from the bacon and hitting his bare skin, but if he wasn't going to think of a shirt, Brandy certainly wasn't going to suggest it.

"I think it's my name," Brandy told him shyly.

He listened carefully and chuckled. "I do believe that it is."

It was a heady little picture they were creating. As if they were a family. A normal family, not with maids and chauffeurs and chaperones and nannies, but just a typical family who liked being together.

Or was that a typical family?

Over pancakes, she threw out her invitation, casually. "Since you cooked breakfast, how about if you let me look after dinner?"

"Sure," he said, easily, as if he had no idea it was going to be the most important dinner of his life and hers.

She was scared to death.

All she knew was that when Clint left the kitchen an hour later to go shower, Brandy felt a song in her heart that was deeper and more wondrous than anything jumping off the edge of a waterfall had ever made her feel.

* * *

Clint, safely sequestered in his office with a back load of paperwork, listened to the steady roar of the vacuum cleaner. He wondered if the engine could burn out from overuse. He had shown Brandy yesterday, in the change room, how to vacuum up all that baby powder. As soon as breakfast had finished this morning, she had hauled his vacuum back out. She'd also found one of those baby carriers that strapped on like a backward backpack and had the baby with her.

Three hours later, she was still at it, energy sizzling in the air around her. If she was like this about vacuuming, what was she like before she took one of those famous leaps off a cliff?

His stomach dropped thinking about it.

The sound of the vacuum changed, and he realized, stunned, it was coming from outside. Sure enough, when he looked out his window, there was Brandy, tongue caught between teeth, hair long since fallen out of its clip, blissfully vacuuming the leaves and debris off his patio.

He opened the window to call to her that the vacuum wouldn't survive outdoor use, when suddenly the engine cut.

She had her cell phone in hand.

Who was she calling? The boyfriend? Not that he intended to eavesdrop, but his window was open, and he could hear the beeps of her dialing the number.

He could not believe the relief he felt when her clear voice said, "Jessica King, please. In class? Tell her it's her sister Chelsea calling. Emergency."

Now he was intrigued. Why was Brandy pretending to be Chelsea?

He didn't have to wait long to find out.

"Hi, Jessie. Yes, Brandy. I wasn't sure if you'd come to the phone for me again, so I said I was Chelsea. Don't hang up!"

He smiled despite himself. He had always enjoyed the antics of the three sisters, appreciated their closeness and their deep love for one another. Somehow, he knew it was that ingredient that had saved them all from becoming typical spoiled monsters.

Jessie was the least flamboyant of Jake's daughters, as smart as a whip. Clint had actually thought she had the greatest chance of achieving some kind of normal life until he'd met her beau at a company function.

Jake had asked him, out of the side of his mouth, what he thought, and Clint had decided it would not be wise to turn his analytical skills on the daughters. Besides, from the look on his face, Jake already knew that Jessie had somehow found herself a complete pompous ass. Clint had shrugged noncommittally; Jake had said that was answer enough, and walked away scowling darkly.

Jessie, who had a degree in science, was telling her sister how to bake potatoes and grill steaks.

He hoped Jessie ditched the guy.

"So," Brandy said, "guess what I was doing before I called you."

Pause.

"Vacuuming! The whole house. Now I'm doing the

outside!" There was a long silence. "Really, Jessie? You can't vacuum outside? But it works so well!"

He had to stifle his laughter. Really, he shouldn't be looking forward to dinner. It was going to be a disaster. He knew that. And still, he was not sure when he had ever looked forward to something so much in his life.

The phone was hung up, and he could hear Brandy dragging the vacuum back into the house, muttering to the baby about how stupid it was that the vacuum cleaner was not built to withstand outdoor use.

Suddenly he felt isolated in this office, lonely. He wanted to be with them, part of that circle of laughter, part of that fresh joy Brandy had in all things.

He looked at his computer screen, listened to her talking. He realized she had put the vacuum away and was going to jump on the trampoline.

He realized he had never once in his life jumped on a trampoline and that it was really about time he started. He turned off his computer, put his papers away, and headed outside.

Chapter Seven

It had been a quiet morning at Jake King's office. Sarah was busy filling out some forms to have duplicate pictures made. Many of the photographs she worked with had all three girls in them and she wanted one copy for each of the three albums.

She glanced over at Jake. He was asleep in his chair, something that happened frequently and that embarrassed him every single time.

Suddenly the office door flew open.

"Daddy!"

Jake jerked awake then grinned with foolish delight as the girl threw herself on him and covered his face with kisses.

Sarah recognized Jake's daughter, of course. It was Chelsea, the youngest. She was the one who was always on the cover of *People* or *Us,* that the *Enquirer* could not get enough of, that *Entertainment Tonight* featured regularly. The public could not seem to get enough of Jake's younger daughter, their favorite American princess.

And yet for all that she had seen Chelsea on TV and in magazines, for all the hours she had spent with her photograph, Sarah was left feeling almost breathless, as if nothing could prepare you to be in the presence of such startling and vital beauty.

Chelsea's blond hair was swept up under an Oliver Twist–style cap. If anything, having that white-blond hair hidden away only emphasized the delicate perfection of Chelsea's bone structure, the soaring cheekbones, the pert nose, the full, pouty lips. She was wearing a camisole-style top, and low-slung slacks that exposed her belly button and showed off her slender curves.

Coming out of her sense of shell shock, Sarah noticed Jake trying to get her attention, and she understood instantly to put the pictures away. The albums were to be a surprise.

She had just slipped the last of them into a box when the smooching was over, and Jake introduced Chelsea to Sarah.

Sarah noticed that whenever anyone came into Jake's office, he always introduced her, as if she were a person of importance, not just part of the furniture. Still, she felt totally intimidated by meeting her aunt. Though they were almost the same age, her aunt was famous. Everyone in the world wanted to meet her. They lined up outside ropes at galas, just hoping to touch her hand.

She braced herself for Chelsea's coolness, for the same snobbery she'd experienced from the maid. But Chelsea bounced over to her desk with all the delight of a young puppy and settled herself on the edge of it. She extended her hand, and her grip and her eyes were both warm as she took in Sarah.

Her eyes were incredible, a stunning mixture of blue and brown that none of the photos Sarah had seen had ever captured.

"How are you, Sarah?" Her voice, like the rest of her, brimmed with confidence and energy. "You look a bit like my sister Brandy. Did you know that?"

"Your father mentioned it," she said, so nervous that her tongue felt glued to her mouth.

"So, what are you doing for Daddy? Some kind of assistant?"

"Something like that."

"Well, he must adore you. I've never seen him let anyone in his office with him before."

Sarah blushed under the unexpected compliment. Of course Jake didn't adore her. He was just a nice old man.

"Chelsea, could you come here for a moment?"

"Ta," Chelsea said and went back to her father.

Ta, Sarah repeated to herself. Who on earth, besides Chelsea King, could get away with that? Ta.

Chelsea and her father bent their heads together and Sarah felt that worm of envy at their obvious closeness. She had never known her father, and the man she had believed was her grandfather could have taught a wild boar the meaning of mean.

Chelsea straightened and looked at her appraisingly.

Then she smiled. "Done," she said to her father. "Sarah, come with me."

Sarah shot Jake a look that plainly said *save me*, but Jake was suddenly engrossed in something else.

She reluctantly followed Chelsea out of the room. Chelsea led her up the winding staircase to the second floor, where Sarah had never been. Her sense of herself as a hick increased as she sank into deep carpets and walked under priceless art, chandeliers dripping crystal that looked as if it were made of diamonds. Chelsea, naturally, noticed none of this, walking along, glancing over her shoulder, chatting about her last trip to Paris.

They came to a door slightly ajar and Chelsea kicked it open, went in and flung herself on the bed. "Oh, it's good to be home," she said, rolling around unselfconsciously on the lace comforter.

The room was like something Sarah might have dreamed, though she doubted if even her dreams would be this rich. The bed cover and the drapes were beautiful antique lace. The bed was canopied in draped silk. Beautiful color photographs of some of the world's most gorgeous people hung tastefully on the walls— Brad, Jennifer, Paris, Britney. Chelsea was in some of them. They were not signed. Friends didn't sign pictures to each other.

What was Sarah Jane McKenzie doing here?

She didn't have to wait long to find out.

Chelsea bounced back off the bed and flung open her closet door.

"Dad heard one of the maids being nasty to you," she said. "He felt bad about it. He had a chat with her—"

That would explain the dagger-like looks Sarah had been getting lately!

"But he didn't know how to make it better with you. Men are kind of dumb that way," she confided. "But don't worry, I know what to do."

"It was nothing, really," Sarah said, backing toward the door. "A misunderstanding, nothing more."

"Humph. Too bad it isn't the olden days. We could have her flogged." Chelsea dissolved into giggles, and Sarah couldn't help the little grin that escaped her.

"This will be almost as good," Chelsea promised. She began to go through her enormous closet, conducting a running commentary. "I love Alessandro Dell'Acqua. Don't you?"

Love him? Sarah couldn't even say his name!

"Vera Wang," Chelsea hummed, "Dolce & Gabbana, Bill Blass. Here." She passed Sarah an armload full of clothes.

Sarah finally got it. Jake had loaned her to his daughter to help clean closets. As long as she got her twelve dollars an hour, did she care? She did. She didn't want to be treated like a maid by the woman who was her aunt.

Foolishly, she longed to be friends.

"Okay, you, in there." Chelsea took Sarah's shoulders and pointed her toward another door.

Sarah stumbled through, feeling as though she were in a trance.

She was in a dressing room, almost like one in a store, only much more posh. There was a hairstyling table and mirrors. There were a couple of big leather chairs.

The door shut behind her.

"What do you want me to do?" she called nervously through the closed door.

"Try on the clothes!"

Sarah looked down at what was in her arms for the first time. Try on the clothes? She wasn't being pressed into closet-cleaning duty? Right on top was a suede jacket as soft as butter and nearly the same color.

"Lucky we're the same size," Chelsea called. "I can tell. Come out and show me everything."

Sarah opened the door and peeked out. "Miss King, I can't, really."

"Oh, posh, get yourself back in there and have some fun with it. Pretend you've won a lottery. And don't ever call me Miss King again."

Sarah stood there, uncertain, and then the girl who was really her aunt grinned at her, and there was really no pity in it, and no charity either, just pure devilment.

Sighing, Sarah went back into the room and shut the door. She tried on the yellow suede jacket with a white shirt and a pair of jeans. All had designer tags in them—Gucci, Zac Posen, Ralph Lauren—names she had seen in magazines or heard tossed out by announcers as celebs went up the red carpet, but that she had never in her wildest dreams thought she would ever wear.

It was just a shirt and just a pair of jeans, but when Sarah turned and looked in the mirror, she understood why people paid such outlandish sums for clothing.

The shirt and the jeans fit like a whisper, clinging in all the right places. They made her look different—taller, more slender, more assured. When she put on the jacket, she didn't look like a pauper from Virginia anymore. She looked like a coed on a college campus, or a young woman who worked in an office.

She took a deep breath and opened the door. Chelsea looked up. She was lying on the bed on her stomach, her legs crossed, heels pointed at the ceiling, leafing through a magazine.

"That's cute," she said, "but you look like a girl who needs to stretch a little. Put on something that's different from what you've ever worn before."

That would be just about anything that cost over twenty dollars, Sarah thought.

"Like those sweet little pink Vera Wang bell-bottoms with the multicolored flared-sleeve shirt."

Sarah tried on the outfit Chelsea had suggested. Her aunt had an eye, all right. Sarah was transformed, instantly, from a poor little church mouse to a sophisticated young woman who would fit in anywhere. A princess.

She showed Chelsea, who nodded approvingly, came off the bed, dug around in her closet and tossed a pair of shoes at her.

"Try it with these divine little Jimmy Choos."

She did. She was suddenly three inches higher. She laughed with delight at her reflection and gave herself over to the pure fun that was being offered her.

She tried on slacks and tops and dresses. She laughed with Chelsea until her stomach hurt.

It seemed like it was an afternoon out of a dream. She had never been one of those carefree girls who was able to while away their afternoons trying on clothes and giggling and gossiping. Impossibly, it seemed as if she could be friends with this lively girl who had grown up in a world so different from her own.

"Here," the door to her change room was opened, and Chelsea threw a dress in at her.

It fell on the floor and Sarah picked it up. There was a discreet price tag, handwritten on a sticker on the back of the designer label that said Monique Lhuillier.

The dress was beautiful—a short black shift, slinky and sequined, with spaghetti straps. Sarah blinked at the price tag. It had cost eleven thousand dollars.

She let go of the dress as if it were red hot, staggered back to the leather chair and collapsed on it.

The tears came, hot, cascading down her cheeks. The more she tried to stop them, the more they came.

"Sarah?"

Sarah sat, trying to stifle the sobs, but she was not successful. The door opened and Chelsea came in.

"Hey, what's the matter?"

"Nothing," she choked out, and then she stood up, grabbing around for her clothes. Unmindful of Chelsea, she slid out of the outfit she had on. She heard Chelsea's horrified gasp at her threadbare underwear, and hastily put on her own threadbare jeans, the too-large sweatshirt with the paint stain on one sleeve that she'd gotten for twenty-five cents at the thrift store in Hollow Gap.

She glanced up to see Chelsea's expression, still frozen in horror from the underwear. She was suddenly aware of the state of her fingernails and the non-style of her lank, dark hair. She stuck her chin in the air, shoved past her aunt and bolted for the door.

She started walking, fast, the fury and shame coexisting inside of her. She walked right out the front door and down the road to the gate, and she kept on going. The road to town seemed long and hard, and she was grateful for every step.

Until the car pulled up beside her.

It was a two-seater yellow sports car. If a dress could be worth eleven thousand dollars, what could that car be worth?

The window on the passenger side slid down.

"Come on, Sarah, get in."

She ignored Chelsea.

"Get in." This time it was snapped, an order from a rich girl who was not used to people not obeying her.

Sarah hesitated then got in the car, a poor girl not used to not obeying. The seats were posh, pure leather, as soft as a baby's skin.

She looked at the road, refused to look at Chelsea.

"Did I do something?" Chelsea asked. "I'm sorry. You seemed to be having so much fun, and then—"

Her agony seemed so real.

"It's not your fault," Sarah told her grimly. "I just want to go home."

"Do you walk to work every day?"

Sarah said nothing.

"I'll drive you home."

"No!"

"But why?"

"I don't want you to see where I live, okay?"

"But why?"

Sarah could not believe people could be so innocent about how the rest of the world worked.

"I don't come from your world," she said. "My mother cleaned people's toilets and never made eleven thousand dollars as a yearly salary in her whole life."

"Eleven thousand? What hat did you pull that figure out of? What's that got to do with anything?"

"That's what that dress was worth. The Monique dress."

Chelsea was silent for a long time. "Oh, Sarah, I'm so sorry."

"I don't want your pity."

"It's not pity."

"Really? What is it then?"

Chelsea was silent. It started to rain.

"Let me out. I'll walk from here."

"No."

She could see from the set of Chelsea's chin, the girl was capable of being every bit as stubborn as she herself was.

"Okay," she said and gave Chelsea directions. "Did you know we're being followed by a blue sedan and a little old man in a suit."

"He's my bodyguard. He'd die if he knew you'd called him a little old man." She giggled, and for a moment it was so infectious, and the idea that Sarah was with someone who had a bodyguard was so absurd, that Sarah wanted to giggle, too.

She gave her aunt directions to the motel. It was a mean little place out of town, off the highway. It needed paint, and some of the letters in the neon sign that blinked off and on were burned out. Once, it had said the Black Cat Motel; now it was the lack Cat. Rooms

Cheap had become Rooms heap. Both were probably more appropriate anyway.

"Thanks," she said stiffly.

"This is where you live?" Chelsea asked in a small voice.

"Yeah." She was aware that her own voice had that tough-girl air to it and that she was about two seconds from crying again. So she got out of the car, slammed the door, went to her own unit right at the end, fitted her key and went in without looking back. You had to slam the door six times, hard, to get it to catch, and, aware her aunt was watching, she didn't bother.

She threw herself on the bed and cried, thinking of her mother working so hard, without a clue that she had sisters who were wearing eleven-thousand-dollar dresses. Carelessly. Giving those dresses as much thought as her mother would have given to buying a box of macaroni. Actually, her mother would have given a lot more thought to that box of macaroni, debating between bargain brands.

The door of her motel room opened, and Sarah rolled over and sat up, hunched over her knees and wrapped her arms around them.

Chelsea stood there, her arms laden with hangers and clothes.

The room wasn't that bad. Everything faded and the paint chipped for sure, but it wasn't dirty.

But Chelsea's expression said she thought it looked very bad. Her mouth was open, and her eyes darted around the room as if she expected a rat to fly out from some dark corner and attack her.

"Ohmygod," she said. "Sarah, you pack up your stuff this instant. You are not staying in this dump one more night."

"Oh, yeah? Where am I staying then?"

"There's an apartment above the garage out at the estate. No one uses it. No one lives in it anymore."

Sarah knew she had to refuse, but she found herself getting up and packing her things. Her hand closed over the ashtray she had stolen from Jake and she turned to see if Chelsea had noticed, but Chelsea was still standing there, with the clothes, frozen as if she were scared to move or touch anything.

It would be dumb to go with her, and yet Sarah felt powerless over the emotion within her.

It was as if all her life, she had waited for one single person to give a damn about her, to look after her instead of her looking after them.

And it seemed like that person was going to be, amazingly enough, Chelsea King.

Brandy laid the last of the silverware, singing a happy little song under her breath. So far, the day had been like a gift from heaven.

She had not believed it when Clint had joined her and Becky on the trampoline. How he had made her laugh, and ooh and aah, doing crazy flips, letting go, having fun.

And now the best was yet to come. Time alone with him. The baby was already in bed, fast asleep.

Brandy surveyed the table with delight. She had unearthed candles, a tablecloth, some decent china. The table was set for two. Originally, she had set it with one setting at each end of the table, but that had seemed just a little too formal. She had switched the settings, so her plate was now just to the right of his, and it looked so much cozier.

The potatoes were baking in the oven, according to Jessica's directions, and the steaks were now thawed on the countertop, ready to grill. The salad, also prepared according to Jessie's instructions, was tossed with a homemade dressing that had been simple to make. Dessert was instant pudding mixed with phony whipped topping. It had been easy and looked exquisite in its layers of dark, light, dark.

Unfortunately, when she looked down at herself, she was wearing quite a bit of the dessert on her shirt, plus there were a few mystery stains compliments of the baby.

She wanted to change anyway. Girl clothes were called for. She glanced at the clock. She had kicked Clint out of the kitchen right after they'd fed the baby and told him not to return until eight. She was so organized, she had time to spare! Almost an hour to go change, maybe do something with her hair.

She'd just run over to her cottage and change into something very sexy. Casual, but sexy. Those new white hip-riding flares and the copper-colored suede-looking shirt that brought out the highlights in her hair.

A loud popping noise from the direction of the kitchen startled her. It was followed by another one. She put her head in the kitchen door, but nothing seemed to be amiss—unless you counted the rather large mess she had left, which she didn't.

Assuring herself everything was under control in the

kitchen, she raced down the path to her cottage. She changed into her outfit of choice and did an experimental whirl in front of the mirror. She realized, deeply satisfied, that she looked about as beautiful as she was ever going to look.

And it had nothing to do with the outfit, as understated and sexy as it was. No, it had everything to do with the healthy glow in her cheeks, caused from a day bouncing on the trampoline in the sunshine. It had everything to do with the deep, contented glow in her eyes.

She licked her lips to make them sparkle even more than the gloss she had applied. Very kissable, she decided.

And then she dug through her things and found her tiniest bikini—much smaller even than the one she had experimented with at fourteen—wrapped it in a towel and headed back to the main house.

As soon as she walked in the door, she knew something had gone drastically wrong in the few minutes since she had left. The kitchen was filled with the acrid smell of something burning. Little wisps of black smoke were curling out the oven door.

She raced to the oven and threw open the door. A cloud of evil-smelling smoke enveloped her. When it cleared, she saw where once there had been potatoes, there was now nothing. The oven racks were empty.

But on the bottom of the stove, chunks and bits of potatoes were sitting on the element, glowing red hot and sending out yet more of that foul smell.

"My potatoes exploded?" she asked herself. She remembered the loud popping noise she had heard earlier.

Glancing at the clock, she didn't know if she had time

to cook more or not. What if she upped the temperature Jessie had suggested?

She did that, but the mess of exploded potato in the oven began to smolder with a fury, and the stink in the kitchen increased. She was going to have to clean that out and then start again.

She opened the oven door and peeked in. It was going to be a bigger job than she had time for. Still, what choice did she have? Hesitantly, she reached in with a spoon, hoping to scoop out the majority of the mess. She almost immediately burned her arm, just above the wrist, on the hot oven rack. Sucking on the incredibly painful burn line on her arm, Brandy decided there had to be a better, faster, safer way to do this.

Inspiration struck! What if she used the vacuum cleaner?

Moments later, she was feeling restored to her happy frame of mind. The vacuum was a superb exploded-potato cleaning tool. The oven had been restored to its pristine condition, and she put new potatoes in to bake at a higher temperature.

She turned on the fan above the stove and then searched the house for every fragrant candle she could find. She soon had them all burning in the kitchen, plus she had borrowed the strawberry-fields bathroom air freshener and generously doused the air with that, too.

She had just finished when Clint walked in.

He quirked an eyebrow at all the candles.

"Don't worry," she said. "It's not about romance. I had a bit of a mishap. Of the smelly variety."

"We're used to that in this house." Was he relieved

that it wasn't about romance? Or disappointed? She couldn't read his expression.

Still, she was very pleased with his appearance. Dress at the lake was very casual, but tonight he was wearing dress slacks, a pressed white shirt, open at the throat, a nice sports jacket. His attire said that it mattered to him that she had gone to all this trouble. That it mattered to him and that somehow he understood it was an important occasion.

He sniffed the air, and she could tell it took him effort to keep his face carefully neutral. And his voice, when he asked casually—much too casually—what they were having for dinner.

Despite all his effort, he looked worried!

"Is that a burn on your arm?" he asked.

"Oh! It's nothing. I accidentally touched the oven rack."

He came over, and she tucked the arm behind her back. Ever so gently, he reached behind her and took it, studied it. "That looks like it hurts."

He dropped her arm back down.

It didn't seem to hurt now, at all!

"It's nothing."

"You poor kid." He turned away from her, retrieved a first-aid kit from the cupboard above the stove. "Sit down for a minute."

She sat down, but mutinously. *You poor kid?* That was the last thing she wanted! His pity! To be seen as a kid!

When she got him in that hot tub, it was going to be a different story!

He knelt in front of her, picked up her arm again, ever so gently cleaned the burn and then, unexpectedly, lifted it to his lips, kissed it.

Her breath stopped. It was something you'd do for a kid, kiss it better. But the look in his eyes was not one reserved for a kid. A light burned hot in them. He dabbed on a bit of ointment and then got up, put the kit away.

"Anything you'd like me to do?" he asked, turning back to her.

Oh, yeah. She had a little spot on her neck that needed a kiss. And one behind her ears, and one on her lips…

"To help with dinner?" he said with a grin.

"Yes, please," she said, bolting out of the chair. "Could you go light the grill?"

He did. She opened the oven door and scowled at the potatoes. The skin was turning an unbecoming color of black. She turned the temperature down marginally, joined him on the deck with the platter of steaks.

The stars were winking on in a dark velvet sky. Across the lake, they could see the lights of other houses coming on.

"This is a beautiful, beautiful place," she said.

"I love it here."

"Did Rebecca like it?"

He smiled. Sadly? "No. I think she only came here once."

"Didn't she decorate the nursery?"

"No. A decorator did."

A stupid thing to feel happy about. But since the name had come up, Brandy wanted to know more. He didn't talk about her. But if he had not gotten over Rebecca, her plan for tonight was a fizzle before it even started.

"Do you miss her, Clint?" she asked softly.

He sighed, faced the lake, his back to her. She wished she could see his face, but she realized his hands on the railing were tense.

"I failed at marriage, Brandy," he said softly.

"What?"

"We weren't happy."

"You weren't?"

"I tried everything I knew." He laughed with a chilling kind of self-scorn. "I even read some books about trying to build a relationship. You see, I never learned anything like that when I was a kid. My home was a battleground between my parents."

"I'm so sorry."

"Don't be sorry. Growing up in that kind of world gave me all kinds of strengths. But one of them was not relationships."

"What was wrong?" she asked, pressing, though she didn't know why, sensing this was important.

"I felt cold and alone, more cold and alone than I've ever felt in my life. It was the exact opposite of what I had expected to feel in my marriage, but I couldn't connect with Rebecca. No matter what I tried."

"I met Rebecca once or twice," Brandy said carefully. "Did it ever occur to you she might not have wanted connection? She was a very self-contained woman."

"I can't blame the failure of my relationship on my dead wife," he said harshly.

"Not even if it's true?"

He was silent for a long time. And then he said, "I accept full responsibility for it."

Some instinct moved her toward him. She touched

his arm and looked him full in the face. She felt how agonized he was by failure.

"Oh, Clint," she said softly. "You feel responsible for everything in the whole world, don't you? Not even you are strong enough to carry the weight of the whole world on your shoulders."

He said nothing.

She continued, softly, strongly, "Rebecca believed what you showed the world. She believed you were a warrior—strong, formidable, aloof. She saw a man who would be willing to lay down his life to protect what mattered to him. I wonder why she felt she needed such protection? I wonder why?"

"Rebecca didn't talk about her childhood, but she let the odd clue slip. Maybe some bad things happened to her, too."

"Things that prevented her from wanting what you wanted, Clint. Connection. A soul mate."

He was watching her now, his eyes fastened on her face, *wanting* to hear what she was saying.

And so she said it. "I see the warrior, too," Brandy admitted, never taking her hand off his arm or her eyes off his face. "But it's lonely, isn't it, Clint? Where do you go when you need a soft place? Where do you have that you don't have to be strong all the time?"

He was silent; he shifted his gaze to the stars.

"Me," she said, risking it all. "When you want to lay down your sword, Clint, when you want to let down your guard, you have me."

He turned and looked at her. His face softened and he reached out, slid his hand tenderly down the line of her jaw to her chin. His thumb rested, for a moment, on the fullness of her bottom lip, and she reached out her tongue.

He yanked away.

She stared at him, hurt, until she saw how he was focused on something in the house.

"Is something burning?" he asked, striding toward the house.

She looked at the smoke curling off the heating barbecue. "That?"

"No."

"Oh, probably just potatoes," she said. Those stupid potatoes were going to wreck one of the most crucial moments of her life. The second set had probably exploded!

But he kept going toward the house. She followed him. He paused in the doorway, lifted his nose to the air.

It did smell in here. A terrible burning odor. Worse than the potatoes had been, though she had not a doubt some crumb had reignited in the bottom of the oven, or that her higher-temperature idea for the second set of potatoes had not been such a good one.

"See?" she said. She went over to the oven and opened the door. No smoke came out. The potatoes in there were looking crispy, but the acrid smell filling the room was not coming from them.

Clint disappeared out the kitchen door into the adjoining hallway. A moment later there as an explosion of curse words.

Brandy raced into the hallway.

Clint was running to the front door with a flaming vacuum cleaner held out in front of him. He opened the door and pitched it out, then turned and folded his arms across his chest.

If she'd ever had any doubt he was a warrior, she did not have it now!

"What happened to my vacuum cleaner?" he asked sternly.

She hung her head and traced a little pattern in the carpet with her toe. She told him about the exploding potatoes and how she had solved the problem by vacuuming them out of the oven.

"I guess combined with the leaves you vacuumed up earlier, that made for a pretty good chance for a fire."

She dared glance up at him.

His lips were twitching. And then he threw back his head and laughed. He came across the room, picked her up and twirled her around, until the whole house rang with their laughter.

They ate steaks, and tried the potatoes, which were partly raw, burned on the outside, and not improved by a few minutes in the microwave. Thank goodness there was plenty of dessert.

They laughed and talked like the oldest of friends. Some barrier had been let down between them.

She knew it was now or never.

"Clint, let's go enjoy the hot tub."

The laughter left his face abruptly. "The hot tub?"

"You know, the one out there on the deck. It's a beautiful night. We could look at the stars."

"Brandy, it's not a good idea."

"Why not?"

"Brandy, you are a beautiful woman, but—"

She held up her hand. "You are not allowed to add *but* to the end of that sentence."

He smiled, tentatively. "Okay. You are a beautiful woman. I am scared to death to get in the hot tub alone with you."

"You see?" she said with satisfaction. "I told you there was a place you could go when you don't want to be a warrior anymore. When you are afraid. That place is me."

"Even if it's you I'm afraid of?" he asked.

"Especially then."

Chapter Eight

Clint took his time in his bedroom. Dinner had been a disaster, an unmitigated disaster from beginning to end. The smell in the house from the flambéing of the vacuum cleaner had been appetite killing, which might have been a blessing. The potatoes had been inedible, the steaks scorched, the salad wilted because Brandy had put the dressing on it sometime in the afternoon. There had been plenty of dessert—chocolate pudding with mysterious powdery lumps in it, layered with dessert topping that tasted as if it had come from a box that proudly proclaimed, *This is an edible oil byproduct."*

For a man with his humble beginnings, it always amazed him how he had come to dine with kings. American kings, anyway. Financial wizards. Business geniuses. Movie stars. Politicians. Clint McPherson, a boy from a very bad neighborhood, had learned from watching carefully which fork to use, how to push the soup spoon toward the outer edge of the bowl, and to never, ever tuck the pure white linen napkins into the front of his shirt.

He, who had grown up on the staples of poor people—potatoes, macaroni, hot dogs, ground beef—had dined on lobster, escargot, filet mignon and other dishes so exotic and delicious they could barely be imagined. And yet he could not remember ever having enjoyed a meal quite so much as the fiasco he had just survived, burning vacuum cleaner notwithstanding.

His lawn had scorch marks on it after all. He had always known that if you got close enough to Brandy King, it was going to be like touching a flame. What he hadn't allowed himself to know before was how intoxicating that experience might be.

It was craziness to go down there to the hot tub with her. It was absolute insanity.

But it seemed to him he had been sane all his life, and it had led him only to loneliness—all his rational decisions, all his careful planning had left no room for spontaneity, for the absolute pleasure of life unfolding in unexpected ways.

The fact that she had recognized his loneliness resonated deeply with him.

As soon as she had said those words—all of them, with her hand on his arm—that place that had always felt so damned empty had begun to fill.

So, was it insane to join her? When he was feeling things he had never allowed himself to feel before?

Yes.

Would that stop him? No.

He felt powerless over what pulled him toward her.

And for a man who had always exercised so much power, it was a relief to feel that way—slightly out of control.

Soon, he would find out if the world would end if he relinquished his legendary hold on it.

He pulled a bathrobe over swim trunks that seemed altogether too much like what Sober-sides would wear.

He went downstairs. She was on the patio, nursing a coffee, looking at the stars.

When she smiled her welcome, he felt again the delicious pull of her and the helplessness he felt in the face of it. She had a huge towel wrapped around herself. It was about as revealing as a burka. But what was under it?

Did he hope for a Speedo? Tank style, athletic, not too revealing?

Of course he did not.

He pulled back the cover of the hot tub, turned on the jets.

"You first," she said.

He yanked off the robe and hopped in the water. It was better to get in it slowly. He felt like he had scalded himself. But somehow this whole situation was rife with danger that wouldn't be improved if she looked at him now the way she had this morning, with hunger turning the innocence of her sapphire eyes to passion.

She got up and came to the edge of the hot tub. She stuck her toe in, her eyes never leaving his. He wanted to look away and found he could not.

She let the towel fall.

A gasp escaped his lips. Because it was not Brandy, the tomboy princess who stood there.

It was a nymph from the sea—perfect, sensual, enticing.

The bathing suit was handkerchief small and constructed of jade froth. He thought it was probably going to melt if she got it wet.

A gentleman would suggest she didn't. But he wasn't really a gentleman. He had been taught how to act like one, but he had never completely banished the outlaw who lurked just beneath that facade of civilized dress and behavior.

He watched wordlessly as she adjusted a tiny little strap that held the skimpy bottom half of the bathing suit in place. She was so much a woman, her curves and lines luscious and soft.

Despite the steam rising off the water, his throat felt dry.

She sat down on the edge of the tub, slid in with slow sensuality.

He knew she was not a kid anymore. She was a full-grown, full-blooded woman. He was not sure when he had ever been so glad about anything.

"It's hot," she said conversationally.

Now that was an understatement!

She had slid into that water and settled on the resin bench right beside him. She wasn't quite touching him, and he was aware he was holding his breath. Then her hand found his thigh.

He tensed, debated, surrendered. He touched hers back and nearly groaned out loud.

Her skin was beautiful, silky, taut. Her eyes never left

his face, and he saw in them what he had always seen that the rest of the world had not.

He saw she was afraid.

"Do you want to kiss me?" she whispered and her voice trembled.

Years ago, when she was nineteen, she had not asked.

She had caught him off guard, captured his lips with her own, offered him something that he'd had to refuse.

But refusing had been god-awful hard. Because he had tasted her fire, and wanted more. Wanted more with a singular kind of desperation that he had not felt before—or since.

It was that want—fierce, wild, untamable—that had fueled the harshness of his reply.

The words he had said to her were burned in his mind. "Miss King, there are some things your money cannot buy."

He had said it with contempt that she had never known was contrived. He had said it with fearsome coolness, driving her away, hurting her. He had not wanted to leave her with even a hint of what he had felt. He'd wanted to crush any hope she'd held that he might ever return what she'd been feeling.

She had been nineteen years old, young, naive, innocent. The seeming boldness of that kiss had not fooled him. She had a life that she needed to live, and if he'd accepted her invitation that night, it would have altered that life. And his. Forever.

But everything was different now, and maybe especially him.

Because he did not want her to be afraid anymore.

She had lived life now, squeezed more activity into the last seven years than most people managed to squeeze into a lifetime. Though she seemed to have retained a lovely quality of childlike wonder, she was not a child.

She had not found the happiness he had wished for her, silently, that night as he had watched her move away from him, her shoulders stiff with pride and hurt.

"Yes," he said gruffly. "I want you to kiss me."

She did.

Her lips were beautiful, questing, shy. She tasted a bit like strawberries and a bit like mint, but mostly like heaven.

He let her take the lead, and she took it easily. The shyness dissipated from the kiss, melted, like snow being touched by lava steam.

He opened his mouth to her. Her hands tangled in his hair, pulling him deeper to her. The tip of her tongue teased his teeth.

He became aware of the wet length of her body pressed against him, as slippery, warm and sensual as the heated oil used by a masseuse.

He wrapped his own arms around her, pulled her close, accepted all that she offered.

The kiss was everything she had promised. Her body was in it, but so was her soul. It was exactly as she had said it would be.

All his life he had looked for the place where he could lay down his sword.

And finally he had found it.

His bones were melting, his muscles. Somehow they dipped below the surface of the water.

They came up, shaking water off their hair and

laughing. She splashed him. He splashed her back. They chased each other around the tight confines of the tub, and then around the deck and then around the yard. They kissed, broke apart, kissed again.

Breathless and shivering, they got back in the tub, into its welcome heat.

She looked at him, touched her fingertips to his lips. "I'm scared," she said.

So, finally, she gave him the gift of herself. Finally, she laid out her truth before him.

He would be worthy of it.

"Me, too," he said huskily. And it was true. This was a fragile thing that had been given to him. How easy it would be to make a misstep, to break it.

With every ounce of his power, he put her away from him and took up his sword.

For a little while, before he accepted what was in her eyes, on her lips, he would be what he had vowed to Jake King he would be: a man of complete honor.

He would have Jake's daughter, for he could not imagine life without her. The prospect looked as empty and cold as the barren lands on a January night. But before things went any further, he was honor bound to let Jake know.

It was not so much that he was asking his permission, because he was pretty sure his own heart had gone beyond that.

But what if Jake didn't approve? What if he would not give his blessing?

Clint shivered, despite the warmth of the hot water around him, despite the warmth of his encounter with Brandy still heating him from within.

But every single thing from this moment forward had to be up front, crystal clear, ringed with absolute integrity.

If he looked at her again, touched her, worst of all accepted the invitation of her lips, his resolve would be gone as thoroughly as sugar into hot coffee.

He looked at her, at the soft glow in her eyes, and he knew her truth.

And he knew his own.

"Brandy," he said, "I can't do this. Not right now."

He lifted himself from the hot tub, looked back at her, crouched and touched her shoulder. "Trust me," he whispered, and then he left her.

Trust him? Brandy stared up at the stars, trying not to cry. She was so sure this time it was going to be different. She was so sure of what she had seen in his eyes.

For a moment, it had felt as if she'd held the whole universe and all its secrets in the palm of her hand.

And then that moment had ended with startling swiftness.

He had rejected her again.

Trust him. Right. She was a girl who had watched her mother get in a car with a handsome young stranger who was not her father and never come back.

The handsome young stranger had been their secret, her and her mother's, until her mother died that day in a terrible crash. And then the whole world had known.

Trust? No, trust did not come easily to Brandy King.

Well, she had come to Clint's hideaway on the lake looking for an answer. This was not the one she had hoped for.

But she knew all about outrunning pain, and there was an island on the very top of the world, a place cold enough that it would be safe to take a frozen heart there, waiting for her.

Clint had never needed her! She had believed what she'd wanted so desperately to believe.

She had made an utter fool of herself, burning steaks and vacuum cleaners, fueled by her stupid desire to be needed by him.

Tomorrow, she would go. She dragged herself out of the hot tub. She carefully pulled the cover back over it, so it would look as if she had left so rationally that she could think of these small details. Shivering with cold, and something else—a kind of forlornness of the soul— she crept back through the darkness to her cottage.

There, in the darkness, she allowed herself to feel the breaking of her heart, and she allowed the tears to fall.

In the morning, she packed her things, tried to put on a face as if everything were okay.

But she never had to use it.

Because Becky and Clint were gone. There was a note on the kitchen table for her. The house felt cold and empty, as cold and empty as her soul felt.

The note was curt to the point of being impersonal.

"Business to attend to. Make yourself at home, back Thursday."

She stared at it. He thought she would wait here? That she was somehow so pathetic and desperate that she would just wait here for him? For a few crumbs of his attention? An opportunity to burn another steak for him? Wreck another vacuum cleaner?

Oh, he would see her again on Thursday all right.

But it would be on a TV news report coming straight out of Baffin Island.

Clint could not help but notice the heat in Jake's office. The old man did not look well, and Clint felt a sudden intuition, and he felt fear.

"This is Sarah," Jake said, and Clint turned to look at the girl who was sharing an office with Jake.

James, Jake's longtime personal assistant, had already had quite a bit to say about Sarah, none of it good, and Clint himself felt an immediate sense of uneasiness.

The girl was quite striking in an understated way, chocolate hair, big brown eyes. But why did the girl look so furtive? Why did her eyes meet his and then slide away as if she had something to hide?

He had barely listened to James's many and varied complaints—including the fact the girl had wormed her way into the apartment over the garage—but now he wished he'd listened more carefully. Later, he would ask his brother, Cameron, who did security for some of the biggest companies and names in the world, including Auto Kingdom, to have somebody make a few inquiries about the girl. For now, Clint had more pressing issues on his mind.

"Sarah," he said, after introductions were complete, "I need a few moments in private with Jake."

He saw a moment's fear in her face. She thought he was going to talk about her. What was she hiding that would make her think that? And how had she managed to circumvent the security checks for the

Kings and Auto Kingdom that Cameron had designed and implemented?

"How's Brandy?" Jake asked, his eyes following Sarah fondly as she closed the office door behind herself. "She looks a bit like her, doesn't she?"

Clint had not noticed a resemblance.

"I actually want to talk to you about Brandy, Jake."

Jake nodded, indicated the couch on the far side of his office.

Clint was taken aback by how much effort it took his boss to get there.

"Are you not well, Jake?" he asked.

Jake waved a hand at him. "I'm eighty-three. I'm as well as can be expected. Tell me about Brandy."

Clint hesitated, wondered how to do this, and suddenly he knew. "You know I garden, don't you, Jake?"

Jake smiled. "I always thought it an odd hobby for you, Clint."

"I know. At times I haven't understood the pull of it myself. It's kind of the opposite of the image everyone has of me. At times it's very much at odds with the image I have of myself—strong, tough, masculine.

"And yet I am pulled to my garden over and over again, I long for spaces of beauty and tranquillity."

He was silent for a time, but Jake didn't push him.

"I've kind of unraveled what it is about gardening that I like, Jake. No matter how I plan that garden, unexpected things happen, usually a whole lot better than what I planned. I guess a garden gives God some room to move. I don't have to be in charge of everything—I just have to plant the seeds, the bulbs, and the miracles happen all by themselves. In the garden, faith brings growth, rebirth, beauty in breathtaking abundance."

Jake nodded, satisfied, rather than surprised.

"Out of that turned-up soil," Clint said softly, "good things come. You see, my garden was trying to tell me something. To hope. To believe. To have faith. To just plant the seeds and everything would be okay—better than I had ever planned it."

Jake nodded, waited.

"In a roundabout way, Jake, I'm trying to tell you I've fallen in love with your daughter. She's made my life into that garden I was talking about."

Jake's head dropped into his hand. Clint realized, embarrassed and saddened, that he was weeping.

"I'm sorry," he said. "I've distressed you. I've betrayed the trust you put in me—"

"Oh, shut up, you foolish young pup."

Clint shut up.

Jake lifted his head from his hand and glared at Clint with the pride of an eagle. "Do you think you are the only one who knows how to plant seeds, who has faith they will grow into something more beautiful than they could ever imagine?"

Clint stared at his boss, stunned.

"I'm dying, son."

"Jake."

"No pity." He held up his hand. "It would unman me. I sent her to you. I knew it would take a man of immeasurable strength to love her, to see her inner beauty, her courage, her spirit, her fragility, her vulnerability. I hoped that man was you."

"You matched me up with your daughter?" Clint sputtered.

"I had hoped for years it would happen on its own, but it didn't. When you married that cold fish—no disrespect for the dead intended—I despaired for you."

"You matched me up with your daughter?" Clint repeated, incredulous.

"I have so little time left, Clint," Jake said, in way of apology. "So little time."

"How much?" Clint whispered.

Jake told him and Clint felt the tears gathering in his own eyes.

"My son, one last request."

His son. Clint's heart swelled. Jake wanted him to marry Brandy. A sudden sensation of absolute freedom enveloped him. All his life, he had harbored the secret feeling that he wasn't quite good enough.

And yet the man whom he loved and respected more than any other had just set him free. He had given him his greatest gift—his beloved daughter. Jake had found him worthy. It underscored a lesson he realized he had been learning this whole past year at the lake, with his daughter. He was a good man. Not infallible, not perfect, but good.

Worthy of that most precious of gifts. The one his daughter gave him. The one Jake gave him. The one Brandy would give him. Love. Clint fought back a sudden desire to leap from his chair, kick up his heels, shout whoo-hoo.

"I wish you hadn't worded it like that."

"Please marry her quickly. So I can see it. So Jessie

and Chelsea can see it. The wonder of it. The magic that is so real all around us. Help them see the miracle, too, Clint."

Clint eyed his friend, his mentor, his soon-to-be father-in-law, shrewdly. Oh, boy. He was planning to do a bit of meddling in the lives of his other girls, too.

Still, that was none of Clint's business. And who knew? Maybe miracles were in the air around Jake right now.

"If Brandy says yes, I'll marry her as soon as the law allows."

"You have quite a bit to learn about women," Jake said. "No King girl, not even the tomboy, is going to say *I do* on the city-hall steps at noon. There has to be some frou-frou around a wedding."

They laughed again, companionable.

The phone rang and Jake scowled at it. "I told James to hold my calls." He picked it up, listened, set it down with a sigh.

"I take it my daughter has not yet heard your declaration of love."

"I felt honor bound to tell you first."

"Ah, well, honor is all well and good but I'm afraid if she keeps at it, that girl may die before I do. She's in Montreal, en route to Baffin Island."

Clint said a word that was straight from the street.

"Precisely," Jake agreed sadly.

It was one of the starkest, most terrifyingly beautiful landscapes Brandy had ever seen.

She had stood on top of the world, on top of a cliff five thousand feet high.

And seeing the beauty was enough for her. The desire to jump was not there.

All her life, she had waited for someone to love her enough to say no. She now realized that person could be herself.

"I'm not going to go," she said, stepped back, laughed out loud. Funny, that freedom would come to her in that way. From saying no, instead of yes.

But that's what she felt—absolutely free of her need to win approval.

"You can't chicken out on me now," Jason said. She had told him yesterday she would not—could not—marry him. Had he seemed relieved that everything was back to buddy status? She thought so. Jason Morehead was not ready to be the man any kind of marriage would require. He was stuck in an endless boyhood.

Just the way she had been stuck until she realized love required more of her.

"Come on, jump," Jason pleaded. "Bok, bok, bok." He made chicken sounds.

But it wasn't about being a chicken. The exact opposite. It was about finding the courage to be herself.

To feel her feelings, all the way through.

Right now that feeling was pain, pain as sharp and jagged as the cliffs rising around her. Pain because she had offered herself to Clint and had been rejected.

She wanted to feel it. She didn't want to hide from it. That pain was a cherished reminder that she had loved deeply.

Did love deeply. It changed who she was in some

way that did not allow her to go back to being the superficial girl she had been two weeks ago.

She turned from the friends who would only accept and care about her if she fit, if she followed, if she did what they were doing.

She climbed into the Bell Ranger helicopter and asked to be returned to the camp.

Looking out the window, as they approached the camp, she saw a lone figure break into a run toward the helicopter pad at the sound of it arriving. She knew who he was. Even when he was little more than a dot on that rugged, ragged landscape, she knew who he was.

Her heart beat in her throat as the helicopter landed and the door opened.

He was coming toward her, his head down. He lifted her out of the door, held her tight.

Neither of them tried to speak over the engines. He set her down, then ducked, his arm on her elbow as they moved away, and the helicopter lifted again.

"Clint, what are you doing here?"

"What do you think?"

"You've come to stop me?" she said mutinously, fighting everything in her that wanted to throw herself at him, bury her cold nose in the warmth of his neck, feel his heart beating, strong, under the layers of his clothing. "Daddy's orders?"

He scanned her face, smiled. "Has anybody ever been able to stop you from doing anything you wanted?"

A big yes, and it had always been him!

"Then why are you here?" she asked.

He leaned close to her. He whispered in her ear.

She reeled back from him, bit down on a mittened fist, stared at him and saw the truth in his eyes.

He loved her.

She cast herself on him with abandon. She kissed his lips and his nose and his eyes, found the curve of his neck, kissed that, too.

Loved!

The sensation was what she had searched for all her life—better than leaping from high places, more real. More lasting.

She looked in his eyes, felt the hardness of his hand on her cheek and knew that this was the thrill that never ended.

There, at the top of the world, he brought her to dizzying new heights. There, in a land that was never quite warm, he gave her the gift of a warmth that never died. There, in a land that knew extremes of light and dark, extremes of danger and hardship, he promised her a place of sanctuary.

He did it with two words.

He said, his voice strong and sure, his eyes lit with deep joy, "Marry me."

She said the one word that made her world right.

"Yes."

Epilogue

Eighty-three years old, Jake thought, and he was having the happiest day of his life.

The wedding had been held here at his beloved Kingsway. His home had been transformed into a fairy-tale kingdom. The house had been in a fever of activity for weeks; menus, caterers, decorators, event planners.

The road leading up to the house had been planted, both sides, with a thousand white rosebushes. The bride, resplendent in a long white gown designed especially for her, had arrived in a horse-drawn carriage. The ceremony had taken place outdoors, in an area made magic by arbors and ribbons and yet more roses. That magic had intensified when Brandy and Clint had looked at each other, exchanged their vows in voices that soared with love and faith and hope.

Three hundred guests had come, all of them cherished by Jake King.

Now the food and the toasts were done. Torches burned, the roses in the reflected lights took on mystical shades of yellow and red and gold and copper. Thousands of small candles and lights burned among the shrubbery. The chairs and tables had been cleared away, and the string orchestra began to tune their instruments.

Jake was surrounded by friends and family. His three girls were together, his new granddaughter, Becky, was fast asleep in her new auntie Chelsea's arms.

He saw the look on Chelsea's face as she looked down at that baby, and he smiled secretively. Perhaps she should be next. She looked ready. He had an idea....

He felt as if nothing could burst the bubble of his happiness.

His eyes settled on Sarah. The child was blossoming like a flower that had needed rain.

He didn't care what James said about her, and it bothered him only slightly that Clint seemed suspicious of her, too. He liked the girl, had liked her from the first moment he had spotted her prowling along his fence like a stray dog looking for a home all those weeks ago. If he had a regret, it was that he had not done enough good things with his life, not changed lives for the better when he'd been given the power to do so.

A sound system clicked to life, and a voice announced that the bride and groom would have the first dance. But it was his favorite music that was played. Ahh. Johann Pachelbel. "The Canon," all of life captured in the sadness and the joy that intermingled so effortlessly in that piece of music.

He watched Clint and Brandy. They might as well have been alone. They were focused so intently on each other, their expressions awe-filled.

And then she left her husband, and came to him, took his hand.

"Daddy."

That blessed word, the reverence with which she spoke it, gave him energy he had not had for a very long time. It took effort to walk from his bedroom to his office these days, and yet his feet had wings that matched the ones on his heart as he danced with his daughter, a married woman.

A little out of breath, he finally took his seat, the tenderness of Brandy's kiss lingering on his cheek. Jake noticed Clint's brother, Cameron, bent over Sarah, and a moment later they were dancing, Sarah beaming in a way that could put the sun to shame.

But what was in Cameron's face? Jake had seen that same look on Clint's face many times—a look that could pierce a person's soul. Clint wouldn't have defied him and asked Cameron, a security expert, to look into Sarah's background, would he?

The thought was like a dark cloud appearing in his happiness and so he brushed it away. He would bask in the love. He would not let anything spoil this evening.

He should have known better than to make such a vow. The gods enjoyed such challenges.

Because suddenly Mitch Michaels, his daughter Jessie's longtime beau, was up at the microphone.

He was wearing that bow tie that both Jake and Clint detested.

"Ahem," he said, and then louder, "ahem."

The dancing stopped, the music petered out awkwardly and everyone turned to face him.

"Jessica, would you join me?"

She was looking spectacular tonight, not as understated as was her norm. The green bridesmaids' dresses, chosen by Chelsea, brought out the incredible color of her eyes, showed off the figure that she usually hid in box-like suits.

Her hair, which she had recently cut far too short and was usually flat as if she wore a toque to bed, had been coaxed into a riot of wheat-colored curls, probably also courtesy of her younger sister. Jessie was twenty-four but she usually looked forty.

Not tonight.

She stepped nervously to the podium beside Mitch. She hated attention. Didn't Mitch know that? Jake didn't like the way Mitch was looking at Jessie, as if he'd seen her for the first time.

"Jessie and I would like to announce our upcoming marriage," Mitch said.

Jessie fought hard to keep the stunned expression off her face. It matched the rather stunned silence that fell over the crowd. Jake glanced over to see Chelsea and Brandy standing frozen.

Someone, who didn't know better, began to applaud politely, and soon the applause rang out in the night air. Jessie accepted a kiss, but couldn't get off that podium fast enough.

Jake's hand was forced. He knew now that Jessie would be next in his matchmaking schemes. She had to be. Because he was not letting his precious daughter marry that pretentious ass.

"Not over my dead body," he muttered, a vow made much stronger by the fact that soon he would be just that, a dead body. He looked again at Brandy and Clint, at the happiness that glowed softly in their faces, and he took strength from that.

Later, much later, after the orchestra had been replaced by a rock band, the festivities halted for another time-honored tradition. Jake was glad that he had not given in to the weariness that tempted him toward bed. He was glad he'd waited to see this moment.

Women and girls formed a loose line, chattering, giggling, an air of eagerness charging the air around them. Chelsea was in the front row, hamming it up. Jessie, he saw, was trying to hide near the back. Brandy stood with her back to them all. It was obvious she had no idea where either of her sisters—or anyone else—had ended up in the cluster of femininity behind her. Then she tossed the bouquet over her shoulder, and she didn't peek.

It sailed high, but with the accuracy of an arrow that had been aimed, it fell straight toward Jessica. For a moment, it looked like she might step back from it and let it fall, rather than catch it. But then, tentatively, she reached out.

The bouquet fell into her waiting hand as softly as a bird finding its nest. She stared at it, incredulous.

"Don't worry, Jessie," Jake promised her softly. "I'm getting really good at this."

* * * * *

Don't miss Jessica's story,
CHASING DREAMS (SR #1818).
Available June 2006!

If you enjoyed what you just read,
then we've got an offer you can't resist!

Take 2 bestselling love stories FREE!

Plus get a FREE surprise gift!

Clip this page and mail it to Silhouette Reader Service™

IN U.S.A.	IN CANADA
3010 Walden Ave.	P.O. Box 609
P.O. Box 1867	Fort Erie, Ontario
Buffalo, N.Y. 14240-1867	L2A 5X3

YES! Please send me 2 free Silhouette Romance® novels and my free surprise gift. After receiving them, if I don't wish to receive anymore, I can return the shipping statement marked cancel. If I don't cancel, I will receive 4 brand-new novels every month, before they're available in stores! In the U.S.A., bill me at the bargain price of $3.57 plus 25¢ shipping and handling per book and applicable sales tax, if any*. In Canada, bill me at the bargain price of $4.05 plus 25¢ shipping and handling per book and applicable taxes**. That's the complete price and a savings of at least 10% off the cover prices—what a great deal! I understand that accepting the 2 free books and gift places me under no obligation ever to buy any books. I can always return a shipment and cancel at any time. Even if I never buy another book from Silhouette, the 2 free books and gift are mine to keep forever.

210 SDN DZ7L
310 SDN DZ7M

Name	(PLEASE PRINT)
Address	Apt.#
City	State/Prov. Zip/Postal Code

Not valid to current Silhouette Romance® subscribers.

Want to try two free books from another series?
Call 1-800-873-8635 or visit www.morefreebooks.com.

* Terms and prices subject to change without notice. Sales tax applicable in N.Y.
** Canadian residents will be charged applicable provincial taxes and GST.
   All orders subject to approval. Offer limited to one per household.
   ® are registered trademarks owned and used by the trademark owner and or its licensee.

SROM04R   ©2004 Harlequin Enterprises Limited

COMING NEXT MONTH

#1818 CHASING DREAMS—Cara Colter

Book-smart and reserved, Jessica King instinctively knows she needs someone to bring her inner wild child out. And though she's engaged to a somewhat stuffy academic, something tells her that earthy mechanic Garner Blake, whom she has just met, may be more the man of her dreams.... But can she find the courage now to listen to her heart and not her head?

#1819 WISHING AND HOPING—Susan Meier

Word on the street is that Tia Capriotti is suddenly marrying Drew Wallace, a longtime neighbor *and* her father's best friend. But inquiring minds want to know—is there something political afoot in their courtship? And what is that subtle bulge at her belly?

#1820 IF THE SLIPPER FITS—Elizabeth Harbison

Concierge; browbeaten orphan—they might be one and the same, with the way Prince Conrad's stepmother treats hostess Lily Tilden in her own boutique hotel. To uncover the jewel that is hers and Conrad's love, Lily must first overcome the royal tricks of this woman, who seems to have studied carefully the wicked women of yore!

#1821 THE PARENT TRAP—Lissa Manley

Divorcée Jill Lindstrom and widower Brandon Clark each just wanted to leave hectic lives and open landmark restaurants in the small Oregon town. But their cooking mixtures seem bland when compared to the elaborate schemes their daughters concoct to give the pair a taste of how delicious their lives could be together....